# Hellfire Canyon

# Hellfire Canyon

*Max McCoy*

**PINNACLE BOOKS**
Kensington Publishing Corp.

www.kensingtonbooks.com

PINNACLE BOOKS are published by

Kensington Publishing Corp.
850 Third Avenue
New York, NY 10022

Copyright © 2007 Max McCoy
Excerpt from *The Last Gunfighter: Avenger* copyright © 2007
William W. Johnstone

All Kensington titles, imprints, and distributed lines are available at
special quantity discounts for bulk purchases for sales promotions, pre-
miums, fund-raising, educational, or institutional use. Special book ex-
cerpts or customized printings can also be created to fit specific needs.
For details, write or phone the office of the Kensington special sales
manager: Kensington Publishing Corp., 850 Third Avenue, New York,
NY 10022, attn: Special Sales Department; phone 1-800-221-2647.

This book is a work of fiction. Names, characters, businesses, organi-
zations, places, events, and incidents either are the product of the
author's imagination or are used fictitiously. Any resemblance to actual
persons, living or dead, events, or locales is entirely coincidental.

PINNACLE BOOKS and the Pinnacle logo are Reg. U.S. Pat. &
TM Off.

ISBN-13: 978-0-7860-1780-5
ISBN-10: 0-7860-1780-5

First printing: February 2007

10 9 8 7 6 5 4 3 2 1

Printed in the United States of America

*For a trio of rebels:*
*David Thompson, Charles Berry, and John Burden.*

*guffed*

### November 7, 1862

At dusk, as a full moon rose in the pale sky above, Alf Bolin stood atop a massive limestone rock on the side of a hill and surveyed the valley below.

"This view," Bolin said, running a hand through his wild red hair, "makes me want to muck somebody up."

The word Bolin said was not *muck*, of course, but it rhymed with it. It was the first time I had ever heard the word uttered with such authority, and I recoiled in shock and fear.

Bolin looked down at me and laughed.

His gang guffawed as well.

There were a dozen of them, and they reminded me of the engravings of pirates I had seen in storybooks—pistols tucked into belts and sashes, knives with blades so large they looked like swords, feathered hats worn at rakish angles. They were scattered about the rock, hidden behind its crags and rounded boulders, lurking in the shadows of a deep fissure that split the highest notch from the lower levels.

"You are a tender thing," Bolin commented from his perch.

He was dressed differently from his gang; instead of the gaudy shirts, the colorful scarves, and the knee-high boots, he wore the simple buckskins of a woodsman. His feet were clad in moccasins. Although he was still in his twentieth year, the elements had turned his face to leather. In the crook of his arm was a half-stock mountain rifle.

"Are you male or female?" Bolin inquired.

"I'm no girl." I self-consciously brushed my blond bangs from my eyes.

"Pity," Bolin said. "Climb up."

"How?" I asked.

The gang member called Vinegar grasped me by the arm and pushed me toward a path that wound along the south side of the rock.

"Follow it up the hillside," Vinegar said. "When you get to the top, you'll be able to walk out onto that top deck as easily as strolling down a sidewalk."

The rock must have been one thing in the long-distant past, but it was now broken into three massive peaks, or notches, with the highest in back. The natural monument was shrouded in trees that still burned with autumn color, and its gray, moss-covered surface had been sculpted by time unimaginable into an object that fired the imagination.

From one angle, the rock looked like the prow of a ship; from another, it resembled a medieval fortress. From yet another vantage point, it suggested the teeth of some subterranean beast gnashing its way through the Ozark soil.

I followed the path, and occasionally had to pull myself up by grasping the trunk of a sapling or scrambling in the dirt. By the time I reached the top, I was panting.

Bolin motioned for me to join him on the rock.

I stepped carefully forward, aware that I was now on a level with the tops of the trees. When I reached Bolin, he placed his right hand on my shoulder.

"Don't be afraid, lad," he said.

Below, I could see the coach road that ran through the valley and came within a few dozen yards of the base of the rock. A series of flat stones stair-stepped down to the road and, with the sun low on the opposite horizon, the light slanted through the trees and glinted from a pool of rainwater.

"How old are you?" he asked.

"Twelve," I said. "No, thirteen. I've passed a birthday."

"A pivotal age," Bolin mused.

"What is this place?" I asked.

"A marvel," Bolin said. "On the third day, when God brought the dry land from the waters beneath the firmament, He placed this rock in Taney County, Missouri. It was here before the sun ruled the day and the moon the night, before the fishes of the sea and the things that creepeth upon the earth, and it was here when man was created from the dust of the ground and woman was taken from the rib of the man."

Bolin paused.

"It was here before we were born and it will remain long after we are dead. This rock is eternal, unchanging, and cares not what we do here. We are as smoke upon it."

I suppressed a shudder.

"Does the rock have a name?" I ventured.

"It used to be called Three Notches," he said.

"What is it called now?"

Bolin held a forefinger to his lips.

"Listen," he whispered. "A team approaches. Do you not hear the music of the harness, the rumble of the wheels, and the clatter of shoes on yonder stones?"

Bolin whistled, a signal to his men, then fell to his belly on the rock and held his rifle at the ready before him. He pulled me down next to him. He swiveled his head to look at me, and his blue eyes seemed to pierce my soul.

"Tell me, young man, what do you desire most?" he asked. "Treasure? Fame? The love of a beautiful girl?"

"Revenge," I said without hesitation.

Bolin smiled.

"Then you are one of us," he said.

Bolin nestled the rifle against his cheek as the wagon neared. It was a Yankee mail coach, a lightweight affair with canvas curtains. Two soldiers, a driver and a guard, sat up front. Bolin eased the hammer back to full cock over the percussion cap, depressed the set trigger, then gently placed his forefinger on the forward trigger.

"Steady, Lucifer," Bolin murmured to the rifle.

As the two-horse team splashed through the pool of rainwater not far from the base of the rock, Bolin fired. The ball hit the driver in the temple and carried the opposite side of his head away, and his body splashed into the puddle.

The guard snapped his Springfield to his shoulder and fired quickly in our direction, and we could hear the minié ball sing through the branches of the trees above our heads. Then he dropped the rifle on the dashboard and reached for the harness reins.

Bolin's gang emerged from a dozen places in the rock, guns firing, and the guard took a round in his right shoulder, dropped the reins, and fell on the far side of the wagon. The team trotted ahead nervously, drawing the wagon ahead a few yards and leaving the wounded soldier with no cover.

"Don't kill him yet," Bolin shouted as he scrambled to his feet, his rifle in one hand and towing me. The path was steep and we scooted down much of it on our rumps, aided by rain-slicked dirt and pine needles.

Two of the gang stood over the wounded Yankee while the rest rifled through the envelopes and packages in the mail coach. They held each item just long enough to determine if it was heavy enough to have something of value, then tossed it over their shoulder onto the ground to find something more promising.

"Where's the gold?" the larger of the guerrillas who stood over the wounded Yankee demanded with a cocked revolver.

"There's no gold, I swear," the soldier said. From the twin chevrons on his shoulder, I knew he was a corporal. The dead Yankee with half a head, whose brains were now steaming in the chill air, had been a private.

Bolin stood over the wounded man. The corporal was old, at least from my point of view—certainly on the far side of thirty.

"Do you know who I am?" Bolin asked.

"Yes," the corporal gasped.

"Then you are acquainted with my reputation," Bolin said.

"You're a monster," he said.

"We are all monsters," Bolin said. "Some of us are simply more direct about it. Tell me, Corporal, if the situation were reversed, would you act any differently than I have?"

"I'm not a murderer."

"This is war," Bolin said, "and war makes murderers of all. But have you ever noticed how the murderers and monsters are always among the *other* side?"

Bolin handed me Lucifer and knelt down to talk to the soldier at eye level.

"You are not badly wounded," he said. "You are much more fortunate than your driver, who has lost a rather important part of his anatomy. He does not miss it, however, since I believe he was dead before he hit the ground."

"Why do you toy with me?" the soldier asked.

"Because it suits me."

The corporal's eyes brimmed with tears.

"I told the captain that it was too risky to try the road around Murder Rock," the soldier said in a broken voice, "but he assured me that it would be safe when the sun went down because the other ambushes have taken place during the day."

"Your superiors have ceased the daylight coaches. We were forced to compensate." Bolin reached down and took a revolver from a flap holster at the corporal's side. "It is a good thing you did not draw this, or you would be as dead as your driver now."

Bolin held the revolver lazily in his left hand as he continued the dialogue.

"And why do you hesitate to kill me now?"

"Because I desire some intelligence from you," Bolin said. "Tell me your point of origin, your destination, and whether you travel with any form of specie."

"No gold or silver," the corporal said. "That is why there was no escort. We set out from Springdale and were on our way to the camp at Forsyth. As your men can see, most of our burden was paper—soldiers' letters home, orders of little consequence, field reports. A few maps."

"You had nearly reached your destination," Bolin said. "Forsyth is just a few short miles to the north. Sadly for you, your commander neglected to take into account tonight's hunting moon, which illuminates our play quite well."

Bolin glanced over his shoulder at the mail coach. The team had been freed and the wagon tipped on its side. Most of the guerrillas were rifling through piles of paper, while one stripped the dead soldier of his uniform and boots.

"So it seems," Bolin said. "And would we find anything of value on your person?"

"A few dollars in coin," he said. "Some cartridges

for the Enfield and some powder and shot for the navy. Some hardtack in my knapsack, beneath the seat there."

"Never developed a taste for it," Bolin said. "Is there nothing else?"

"No," the soldier said.

"Burn the coach," Bolin said over his shoulder.

"But we ain't through with it," one of the gang protested. "I found one helluva letter here from a homesick Yankee to his gal in Indiana. 'My dearest Viola,' the bluebelly says, 'only the memory of our tender moments have sustained me in this wilderness hell—'"

"It's trash. Burn it," Bolin commanded.

The guerrilla threw the letter down and prepared to fire the wagon.

"Jack!" Bolin shouted. "Jack! I have need of you."

"Which Jack?" a guerrilla called.

"Scarecrow Jack," Bolin said.

A painfully thin guerrilla with a baby-blue bandanna over the lower half of his face and a shock of blond hair left the wagon and ran over. He appeared unarmed, except for the bone handle of a straight razor that peeked from the top of the belt around his skeletal waist.

"Why does this one hide his face while the rest of you are undisguised?" the corporal asked with suspicion. "Is he the designated assassin?"

"Show him," Bolin said.

Scarecrow Jack hovered over the corporal, then reached up with bony fingers and jerked the bandanna away. He had no lips and his jagged yellow teeth were exposed in a perpetual grin, a human jack-o'-lantern.

The corporal turned away.

The lipless guerrilla uttered something barely intelligible, but which I recognized after a few moments as:

"Pretty, ain't I?"

Bolin reached out, grasped the corporal's jaw, and wrenched his head back.

"Look at him!" Bolin shouted. "Your comrades along Big River in eastern Missouri carved him so, believing he knew something of the whereabouts of my friend Sam Hildebrand. Jack did, of course, but did not tell."

Scarecrow Jack flicked his pink tongue at the corporal.

"Oh, my Lord," the soldier said.

"Jack, I think this Yankee is lying."

"I swear I'm not."

"We shall soon find out," Bolin said. Then he ran his fingers over the gray stubble on the soldier's face. "I think you need a shave."

Bolin stood and motioned to Scarecrow Jack, who straddled the corporal's chest, his knees pinning his arms, and drew the bone-handled razor. He flicked it open, and the hungry fire consuming the mail coach was reflected in the well-honed blade.

Scarecrow Jack carefully placed the razor against the corporal's throat. The soldier jerked, and blood oozed from the thin red line where the blade had been.

"I would remain still if I were you," Bolin suggested.

Scarecrow Jack frowned—or perhaps he grinned more broadly, for it was hard to tell—and the razor approached the corporal's throat once more. Then he paused thoughtfully, muttered to himself, and moved the razor to the soldier's right cheek. The blade scraped slowly along, neatly removing the sideburn, then flicked downward, slicing away the earlobe.

Blood poured down the side of the soldier's neck.

"Most scream when Jack does that," Bolin commented.

"Would it matter if I did?"

"No," Bolin said. "It would not."

Scarecrow Jack wiped the razor on his sleeve, then positioned the blade beneath the soldier's nose.

"There's something else," the corporal said quickly.

"Oh?" Bolin asked.

"Look in the pocket of my blouse," he said.

"Hold," Bolin said, and Scarecrow Jack withdrew the blade. His long fingers probed the pockets of the corporal's uniform, and finally retrieved a small leather pouch.

He handed it to Bolin.

"Why, this cannot be anything of worth," Bolin said, weighing it in the palm of his hand. "It is much too small. Are you trying to barter your chewing tobacco in order to keep your nose a bit longer?"

"Open it," the corporal said.

Bolin tucked the revolver into his belt and loosened the drawstring of the pouch. He shook the contents into his palm. It looked like a handful of smooth river gravel, but with the sheen of freshly poured lead. Most were the size of peas, but one was egg-shaped and larger than a rifle ball.

"What are these?" Bolin asked.

"Diamonds," the corporal said, struggling for breath.

Bolin looked uncertain. "They feel oily. They are some type of metal, perhaps, or slag."

"Have you never seen a diamond?" the corporal asked.

"These do not resemble gems."

"These are raw, uncut," the corporal said.

"You take me for a fool," Bolin said. "Diamonds are not native to this region."

"That's what I believed as well, until we found a deposit in a plowed field far south of here during a foraging party," the corporal said. "I did not know their worth, either, but my friend had studied geology."

"How far south?" Bolin asked.

"In the mountains well below the Arkansas River," he said. "A place called Murfreesboro."

"And your friend?"

"Died of dysentery," the corporal said.

Bolin picked out the largest stone.

"What of this?"

"The biggest we found," the corporal said. "My friend said it was of excellent quality, and he judged that it was worth a fortune."

Bolin held the stone between his thumb and

forefinger and lifted it to his eye. It caught the moon and emitted a gentle blue light.

"It is like a robin's egg," Bolin said.

"Indeed," the soldier said.

"Who else knows of this?"

"None but us," the soldier said. "I'll take you there, if you wish. There are more to be found. We will certainly be wealthy men."

Bolin laughed as he returned the stone to the pouch.

"Only a fool longs for wealth," Bolin said. "I have butchered dozens who used their last measure of life to hide their pitiful possessions. But none of their gold bought them an extra second of life, or happiness, or comfort."

"Wealth can buy those things," the corporal ventured.

"Not here," Bolin said. "There are no stores to buy pretty things, or fine beds in which to sleep, or handsome and well-born women to impress. What is of value here is a good eye, a steady hand, and health enough to use them. The things that we require—good horses, powder and leaden ball, food enough for a full stomach, and the occasional feminine brace—those things we take."

"Your speech betrays your loneliness."

"I have my men," Bolin said. "A biblical twelve, outcasts and outlaws who follow me by force of my personality, and each is prepared to die for me when necessary. And I would do the same for each of them. But I confess that I long for the company of a woman that would be my equal—a strong woman, with a fine figure, and conversant enough in the world to ponder with me the mystery that is living."

Bolin's ruddy face turned a deeper red.

"Now I have proved myself the fool," he said.

"You have simply proved yourself a human creature," the soldier said with genuine kindness.

"Perhaps," Bolin said. "But a monster I remain."

Scarecrow Jack held out his hands, as if to ask what to do now with the soldier. Bolin said to let him up, and Jack stood, but kept the razor handy.

"Thank you," the corporal said as he struggled to his feet. He placed a hand over his bleeding ear, and his shoulder wound was dripping blood down his uniform sleeve, where it dripped steadily from the cuff.

"Do not thank me," Bolin said, his mood turning dark.

The soldier started to protest, but Bolin struck his face with the back of his hand. The man staggered back a few steps, but remained standing.

"Find some sand," Bolin said. "I have grown to respect you and will be disappointed if you act the coward now. Refrain from speaking now, or bargaining, or telling me your name and that of your wife and children, if you have them. I care not."

Then Bolin turned to me.

"What is the nature of the revenge you seek?" he asked.

My mind was so numb from the spectacle I had witnessed that for a moment I could form no words.

"Speak," Bolin urged as he took back his rifle from my grasp. "What offense has been visited upon you or your family? What is the vengeance for which you thirst?"

"I desire to kill a certain man."

"Why?"

"That is between me and the Divine."

"Was this man a Yankee?"

"Yes," I said. "A provost marshal."

"The Yankees differ only in rank," Bolin said. He drew the navy revolver from his belt and offered it to me butt-first. "You might as well start with this one and work your way up."

I took the revolver in my left hand.

Whatever rage drove Bolin jumped like a spark from the gun and traveled up my arm. It ignited in my chest, and I could feel the pounding of my heart in my eardrums, and my own rage at the losses I had suffered in a few short weeks became a crescendo of hate. My head was on fire, and even though the air was cool, sweat began to bead on my brow.

I drew the hammer back. The cylinder spun and clicked into place. Then I stepped forward with my left foot, extended my arm, and placed the brass bead of the front sight over the corporal's chest.

The corporal clasped his hands.

"Surely you don't mean to have a child assassinate me?" he asked with terror and disbelief. He dropped to his knees, but his eyes remained on the octagonal barrel of the Colt's, which wavered slightly.

"He's not the one," I said. "He does not deserve it."

"All of us deserve it," Bolin said. "Besides, if your aim is true, then he will die quickly. He has earned that much. But if you refuse, then I will turn him over to my scarecrow pet, who will delight in flaying him alive."

Then Bolin leaned so close that I could feel the whiskers of his auburn beard on my neck.

"Squeeze the trigger," he urged, "and you will be a child no longer."

Bogged down

# A Word of Explanation

It was by chance that I stumbled upon the story of the outlaw fiddler Jacob Gamble. For some time I've been the investigative reporter for a daily newspaper in southwest Missouri, and such journalism requires reviewing hundreds or thousands of documents for each story. To ease the tedium, I haunted the newspaper archives in an attempt to locate bits of local legend and folklore. Of particular interest to me was to verify a story that had circulated at the newspaper for years, that one of its editors in the 1930s, in keeping with the hard-nosed image of the craft at the time, had kept a human skull on his desk for use as an ashtray.

I was assisted in this quest by my friend Bill Caldwell, who had maintained the newspaper's morgue for years before the executives decided to discontinue the practice of hand-clipping and filing articles. The reasoning was that in the electronic age, clippings are unnecessary. Not coincidentally, a digital archive would also save money. But the chosen software never worked as promised. Between tech-

nical problems and the inadequate substitution of
Boolean logic for common sense, the newspaper
suffered from chronic institutional amnesia. Even
though Caldwell had been assigned other duties,
frustrated reporters often turned to him for background on any story that exceeded recent memory.

We never located the source of the cranial ashtray yarn, but Bill would often bring me yellowed
clippings of Joplin's arcane past. One day he placed
a thick file on my desk and asked, "Have you ever
heard of *Hellfire Canyon*?"

It was, he explained, an obscure RKO movie that
had premiered in Joplin in the early 1930s. It was
loosely based, he said, on the life of Jacob Gamble,
who as a boy in the Civil War had known the notorious Alf Bolin.

Bolin operated in the Branson area, and is forgotten now by all but a few local historians—and remembered, surprisingly, in a train-robbery skit for
the benefit of the tourists at the Silver Dollar City
amusement park, where Bolin is portrayed for
laughs as a hillbilly buffoon. But the real Alf Bolin
was far from laughable. He ambushed and killed
dozens along the stagecoach road at a limestone
outcrop in Taney County, a few miles from present
downtown Branson, and many historians consider
Bolin to be one of America's first serial killers. Because such terminology had not entered the lexi-
con until the FBI's Behavioral Science Unit coined
it in the 1970s, the contemporary Civil War ac-
counts simply described Bolin as a monster.

"This entire file is about the movie?" I asked,
then opened the file and flipped through several
hundred pages: typed documents, handwritten

notes, and ledger pages that looked like some kind of diary, written in pencil in an old-fashioned hand.

"No," Bill said. "Most of it is in Gamble's own words, written in that fine cursive, and the rest are notes that were typed after a *Globe* reporter named Frank Donovan interviewed Gamble the night after the Joplin premiere at the Orpheum Theatre downtown. He was in his eighties at the time."

I whistled.

"Did the newspaper publish any of this?"

"No," Bill said. "A blue-pencil note from an unidentified editor to Donovan declares that the piece is too long, the interview subject unreliable, and the subject matter unsuitable for the newspaper's readership. All of this work was condensed to a six-inch announcement on an inside page that eighty-three-year-old Jacob Gamble had attended the premiere, expressed his displeasure at the historical inaccuracy, and accused the studio executives of being too stupid to realize there are no canyons in the Ozarks, only hollers."

"Who was this Donovan?"

"Don't know," Bill said. "This is the first I've heard of him, but he had a nice style, judging from what I've read so far."

"Think there's a Sunday story here?"

"There may be more than that," Bill said, and he slid out a page from the manuscript.

*"You don't know me without having been in Missouri during the war, or parts west thereafter. Chances are we have never met. I'm an old man now and even as you read these pages, I may be long dead. But I have some things to say about love and death and the devil. I don't understand everything yet, though soon I might."*

That caught my attention.

"Think there's a book here?" Bill asked.

"Perhaps," I said, flipping through the pages. "But only if I'm talented enough to edit it into a cohesive story. It seems to jump around a lot, and the switch between the 1860s and the 1930s is jarring. It's worth a try, but it might take me a few weeks."

You hold the result.

I was nearly driven mad by attempting to verify dates and places, sometimes bent on proving the manuscript a hoax because of seeming anachronisms, and trying my best to accurately portray Donovan's character through the many interviews, notes, and often indecipherable personal observations scribbled in pencil in the margins of the type-written pages. My own voice is used sparingly, and mostly in the form of footnotes to amplify or interpret portions of the text for modern readers.

*Max McCoy*
*Joplin, Missouri*
*July 2006*

# One

Seventy years pass.

As I write these lines, I am sitting at a window table in the House of Lords Bar on the principal thoroughfare of Joplin, a bloody-knuckled mining town in the southwest corner of Missouri. A glass of whiskey is at my elbow. In my left coat pocket is a .45-caliber Colt automatic, a brutish weapon compared to the elegant simplicity of the cap-and-ball revolvers of my youth, but a handgun that has no equal in pure man-stopping power. Such have become the tools in my line of work.

Outside, the street hums with commerce—horses and wagons and motor cars and the electric trolleys that unite the outlying mining camps with the fledgling metropolis. It is late afternoon and scattered on the sidewalks are the miners, the long-faced men upon whose backs this wealth is built, lunch pails swinging at the ends of lanky arms.

I have never cared much for Joplin, or any center of commerce for that matter, preferring instead the solitude of the deep Ozarks of my childhood.

But I have been summoned here to meet a scribbler for one of the local newspapers, and since consideration is promised, I am happy enough to drown the bitterness with whiskey, watch the thoroughfare, and record my thoughts while awaiting the appointed hour. The reporter, one Frank Donovan, wants the story of my life.

Of course, Donovan will want to know about Alf Bolin.

And I won't tell the truth.

Instead, I will spin the tale that is expected—that I was forced by circumstances at the tender age of thirteen to become the youngest member of the Bolin gang. I will say Bolin was a monster who killed without remorse, that he was an illiterate woodsman with an animal's cunning for the chase and the kill, and that while I was lucky enough to escape with my hide intact, the ordeal set my feet firmly on the path of crime. My only saving grace, I will plead, is that for all my dash and daring, for all of the crimes committed since those dark days in the wilderness, I have never shed innocent blood.

And it will all be lies.

# Two

When I finally met Jacob Gamble, the outlaw fiddler, it was in the House of Lords not half a block from the newspaper office. He was sitting at a table near the window of the bar, sipping whiskey and writing in a neat hand in a ledger book.

Instead of introducing myself right away, I went to the bar, exchanged a few words with the tavern owner, Joe Dorizzi, and gave him a package to keep. Then I lingered at the bar and nursed a cold glass of beer while studying my subject from a safe distance. It was a habit developed in my years of interviewing princes and paupers, and it usually paid off. People's behavior speaks volumes about their approach to the world, and a little observation allows me to tailor my approach to the job at hand.

I knew it was Gamble because he was unmistakably the man I had studied in old photographs—a patch over his right eye, tall and rail-thin, possessed of an almost feminine grace, and with a visage that reminded me of the statue of Moses at the church of St. Peter in Chains at Rome. In other words, he resembled a man whose face radiated with a secret light after meeting with God and living to tell of it. About the only things that were missing were the horns that Michelangelo had placed on the top of the patriarch's head.

The stub of a pencil was clutched in Gamble's left hand, and on the tabletop was a pocketknife that he periodically used to trim the lead to a fine point. He was wearing black, and even though he was in his eighties, he had a full head of long blond hair that had gone gray only at the temples. Every so often, he would peer out the window onto the hubbub of Main Street, and the afternoon light reflected in his one good eye, which was clear and blue.

Soon, he grew restless and glanced at his pocket watch, and I decided it was time to end my study and get on with it. I finished my beer, straightened my clothes, and walked with purpose to the table.

"Frankie Donovan," I said.

Gamble smiled.

"A girl reporter," he said. "You didn't say that in your letter."

"Frank Donovan is my byline," I said. "I don't want to be thought of as just a 'girl reporter.' Besides, would it have mattered if I had identified myself as a woman?"

"Yes," he said. "I would have answered much sooner."

Gamble placed the pencil in the ledger and closed it, closed the pocketknife and placed it in his vest pocket, and stood. His chair scraped on the wooden floor as it was forced backward by the strength of his calves.

I held out my hand, but instead of shaking it, he took it gently in his left hand and brought it to his lips. The kiss was brief enough to remain within the bounds of good taste, but just long enough to be sincere.

"Charming," he said.

I felt myself blush.

Then he moved to pull a chair out for me, but I insisted on doing it myself.

"As you wish," he said, but waited until I had taken my seat before returning to his.

"Why do you dress in men's clothing?"

"Because it is a man's world."

"And you aim to be a part of it?"

"Something like that," I said.

"Then let us behave as men," Gamble said. He drained his whiskey, lifted the glass, and beckoned for another. "You said you wanted to know the story of my life. I gather that the only reason you are interested in me is because of the talking picture."

"It has created a sensation."

I indicated to the bartender that I would have a whiskey as well.

"Have you seen it?" he asked.

"I was at the premiere two nights ago, a block from here at the Orpheum. It was entertaining enough. But I'm curious about how much of the story is true."

"Does it matter?" Gamble asked.

"Of course it matters," I said. "Readers are mad for anything connected to Hollywood, and a local angle is guaranteed sales at the newsstand. It was shot locally, you know—Granby is just a few miles from here."

"I know where Granby is," Gamble said as the Irish waiter brought a tray with two straight whiskeys. The waiter placed the drinks on the table, removed Gamble's empty glass, and waited patiently.

"This one is on my partner," Gamble said.

"Of course," I said, and fumbled in my pocket for a silver dollar and placed it on the tray.

"Keep the change," Gamble said.

The waiter nodded his thanks, then vanished.

Gamble raised his drink.

"Here's to the end of Prohibition," he said.

"So, did you see the picture?" I asked.

"The actor who plays me in the film—what's his name?"

"Tyrone Power."

"Never heard of him."

"He's new."

"Well, he's too old to be playing me," Gamble said. "He must be twenty. So is the actor who plays Bolin. But I liked his performance somewhat better."

"John Huston," I said. "He's thirty. He was born not far from here, in the town of Nevada. He also wrote the script."

"He didn't ask my advice."

"He thought you were dead."

"Well, should have known better than to call it *Hellfire Canyon*," Gamble said. "There are no canyons in the Ozarks—hollers, yes, but canyon is a Western word."

"The movie is a Western," I said. "It was probably named by the studio, to attract the largest audience. Besides, *Hellfire Holler* sounds like a comedy, doesn't it?"

"There was nothing funny about Murder Rock."

"I rather like their title," I said. "It suggests a place where one's very soul is in peril. Good and evil. And that reminds me."

From my jacket pocket I withdrew the ledger pages that Gamble had sent. I unfolded them and placed them on the table between us.

"Is there more?"

"Yes," he said.

"So what happens next?"

Gamble smiled.

"This is a neat bit of fiction," I said.

"It is not a storybook," Gamble said defensively. "I put it down as I remember it. Of course, seventy years have passed, and some of the names and dates escape me now. But the entire account is true."

I nodded toward the pages.

"Do you always write in ledger books?"

"It is a habit I developed long ago," he said. "Ledger pages are lined, and were always much easier to obtain than the blank kind that folks use for letters home."

"This episode," I said, tapping the pages. "It is peculiar. You don't explain what brought you to Murder Rock, or who you wanted to kill, or even whether you pulled the trigger on the poor corporal."

Gamble shrugged.

"It was all I felt like sending."

I did not hide my frustration.

"Let us understand one another," I said. "I'm not some little girl begging for a story at my grandfather's knee. I am a professional in need of a story for tomorrow's paper, and if you are unwilling, you should stop wasting my time."

"Your newspaper," Gamble said, "does not have the space to publish my story."

"Try me," I said. "I'm very good at summary."

"You mentioned consideration in your letter," Gamble said.

"I have something in mind," I said. "But I will make my offer only after I've heard your story. If you find the offer unacceptable, then I agree to print not a word of our conversation."

"Do you play poker, Miss Donovan?"

"From time to time," I said. "From what I've read about you, Mr. Gamble, you don't seem like the kind of man to shy away from a risk."

"Nor do you," Gamble said. "You've been admiring the line of my jacket."

"I recognize the outline of a heater when I see one."

Gamble laughed.

"Heater," he said. "Now, who came up with that bit of slang? These gangsters nowadays, they are spoiled. Thompsons. Guns that spray bullets as if from a fire hose."

"Was it so very different when Bolin and his guerrillas carried braces of six-guns?" I asked. "The typical soldier carried a rifle that could fire perhaps three shots a minute, with expert reloading. You could accurately place a dozen shots in the same amount of time."

"Your point," Gamble said.

"Why do you still feel a need to carry a gun?"

"My enemies are legion," he said.

Before I could ask what enemies, he changed the subject.

"You know, I have disliked the bobbed hair that women have adopted since the last decade," Gamble said. "But, Miss Donovan, it suits you."

"It is a practical matter," I said. "Short hair is easier to care for."

"If people think I am dead," he asked, "how did you find me?"

"I have a friend at the penitentiary at Jefferson City," I said. "He sent me the addresses they had on file when they locked you up. I wrote to all of them."

"Ah," Gamble said.

"Will you tell me your story?"

"Do you have the time?"

"I understand the bar stays open quite late," I said.

"You must promise that you won't publish until I have left the state," he said. "A couple of days should put extradition behind me."

"And don't worry," I said. "I won't tell where you live."

"You don't know where I live," he said. "That letter was forwarded."

I took a pencil and a sheaf of blank pages from my pocket. The papers were folded twice, lengthwise, which gave six clean panels per sheet on which to write. I took a few shorthand notes about some of the things that Gamble had already told me.

Then I sensed that Gamble's mood had changed.

"It's important for you to relax," I said. "Lots of folks get nervous when the pencil and paper come out, but I want you to forget about that. We're just two friends talking."

"You mistake my thoughtfulness for anxiety."

"And what has caused this introspection?"

"The weight of years," he said. "And the fact that much of what I am prepared to tell you I have never confided to another soul. Your readers may find some of it unpalatable. Is that what you desire, Miss Donovan?"

"I desire the truth," I said.

"Then where do you want me to start?"

"At the beginning, of course," I said.

4) unpalatable

(2) Introspection.

# Three

My mother was Eliza Gamble. She was a liar and a thief, wildly superstitious, equal parts gypsy and pirate, and altogether the most courageous woman I have ever known. Together we walked from our farm in Shelby County to the federal prison at Palmyra[1] in one day.

Mother was twenty-six, with flaming hair and ice-blue eyes, and over her dress she wore a man's butternut coat with a .36-caliber Manhattan[2] revolver tucked into the right pocket. I was too young to understand all that happened that day, and for many years after, but now I know that she loved my father and was trying to save his life.

1. Palmyra is the seat of Marion County in northeastern Missouri. The county is named for General Francis Marion, the "Swamp Fox" of Revolutionary War fame. Its most famous city is Hannibal, the birthplace of Mark Twain. Shelby County is immediately west.
2. Manhattan revolvers were copies of the popular Colt navy. About 78,000 Manhattans were produced from 1859 to 1868 at Newark, New Jersey, and many of them were privately purchased by soldiers on both sides of the Civil War.

I was twelve when the guerrillas came to our farm early one morning in the middle of October of 1862, and rousted my mother and me from our beds.

There were three of them. They obviously had been riding all night; their faces and clothes were caked with dust, and their eyes were red from lack of sleep.

Their leader was a fat old man with long gray hair and a full beard, a slouch hat worn at a rakish angle, and a leather necklace adorned with weird-looking scraps of what looked like shriveled and rotting bacon. He demanded breakfast for them all. I huddled in a corner of our rough-hewn cabin as Mother cooked up the last of our ham and eggs.

The fat guerrilla ate greedily. He scooped food into his mouth with the blade of a wicked-looking knife with one hand, while sopping a biscuit with the other. On the table within easy reach was a short-barreled revolver of the kind favored by constables and sheriffs.

Then he paused.

"What is today?" he asked.

"Don't reckon I know or care," the guerrilla nearest the window said.

"It is Friday," Mother volunteered.

She was standing behind them, her hair in a bun, hands in her apron.

"Hell," the fat guerrilla said. "How I despise Fridays!" His face grew somber, and he cocked his head as if listening to a voice only he could hear. "The day they crucified our Lord. Hangman's day in England. The day of the Last Judgment."

"We'd best be on our way, Jack," said the guerrilla near the window.

"Before we've finished our breakfast?" the old man asked. "I'll not greet the devil on an empty stomach." And then he began to mug, as if meeting Satan in person: "Pleased to meet you, Your Highness. Mad Jack Vandiver and company, at your service. Truffles? Why no, we've just ate!"

The third guerrilla was puzzled. He was younger than the others, his hair resembled a bird's nest, and he wore a long butternut coat.

"What're truffles?" he asked.

"Black magic that grows beneath the roots of oak trees," Mad Jack said expansively. "You find 'em by using pigs for bloodhounds, and then you make a Frenchman cook 'em up. The devil has plenty of Frenchies."

While Mad Jack was going on about truffles, the guerrilla who had urged speed was peering out the window.

"Dammit, Jack," he said, still facing the window. "Stop telling the boy lies. You've never had the pleasure of passing truffles through that gut of yours."

Mad Jack snatched up his revolver and pressed the muzzle against the man's temple. The gun seemed like a toy in Jack's broad hand.

"Take that back," he said. "I won't stand for cussing in front of a woman."

The cautious guerrilla rolled his eyes.

"Why do you favor that tiny thing? It's an embarrassment, Jack. You'd be lucky to give me a black eye."

Mad Jack cocked the revolver.

"Let's find out."

The other man glared, but finally relented.

"I beg your pardon, madam."

Satisfied, Mad Jack withdrew the gun.

"Gentlemen," Mother suggested, her hands folded in her apron. "If you're in a hurry, I could wrap your food in damp cloth. It would keep."

"Oh, my digestion requires a sit-down meal," Jack said. "It's not good for your health to eat and run."

"It may not be so healthy *not* to run," the other guerrilla argued.

"Oh, the devil and I have an understanding," Jack said. "He keeps me healthy as long as I keep sending him Yankee souls." Then he grasped the necklace and turned to Mother. "I keep their ears so's I can keep a good account."

Jack scooped some more eggs up with his knife.

"You ought to wash that knife before you eat with it," she said.

"Don't worry," Mad Jack said, then lunged at her while snapping his teeth. "I bites them off."

Mother jumped back as Mad Jack roared with laughter.

He was obviously quite insane.

The cautious guerrilla picked at his eggs and looked around the cabin. He spotted a fiddle hanging from a peg on the wall and asked Mother if she played.

"No," she said. "My husband does. And my son."

"My wife is partial to fiddle music," he said. "I used to play for her, before the war. She sings a little. How I miss her voice."

"I'm sure you'll hear it soon," Mother said brightly.

"The thought cheers me," the guerrilla said. "And if I'm allowed to be so bold, you keep your husband's cabin well. It is not an easy task, here in the wilderness, so far from neighbors. But this cabin reminds me strongly of my own home, and few things would make me happier right now than to pass a few hours sleeping in this safe and happy home."

"You certainly seem in need of rest," Mother said. "There are feather beds in the lofts."

"I'm afraid there is not time now, madam," he said. "It will be many days before we are allowed to sleep."

"Well, upon your next visit," Mother said. "You are gracious and well-mannered and you have a waiting bed here at any time that you need it."

"Thank you," he said. "But I hardly deserve such kindness."

"You deserve that and more," she said. "You are a gentle and handsome man who belongs with his family. I hope the reunion you seek is soon."

"I fear that I may never see them again."

"They say the war won't last long," Mother said.

"Oh, shush," Mad Jack said. "This is great sport. If the war hadn't come along, I wouldn't be enjoying such a fine breakfast with such good company this morning. What's that?" Then he turned to Mother. "Oh, I'm asked to tell you to leave those cards alone for a spell. You've already been told all that you need to know."

"What?" Mother asked.

"Don't pay him any mind," the cautious guerrilla said. "He believes the devil speaks to him. I would say it is all hokum, but the thing is that Old Scratch is right most of the time. Do you play cards, madam?"

"No," she said, flustered. "Of course not."

She wasn't lying, exactly. She didn't play cards. She read the cards in secret, a gift she said she had inherited from own mother, a French-speaking woman from St. Charles who had married a dragoon who was on his way to the frontier at Fort Scott, Missouri.[3]

"What's your name?" Mother asked.

"Mason."

"You seem a gentle person, sir," she said. "What are you doing with such companions?"

He smiled.

"Jack may look like a tub of guts, but he is bar none the best fighter I've ever seen," he said. "The kid is green, and dumb as a stump, but true to his companions. I reckon I could do worse."

The young guerrilla seemed not to mind the insult.

"Do you have more biscuits?" he asked.

"No, I'm sorry," Mother said.

"That's okay," he said. "They were good."

"Thank you," she said.

"More coffee," Mad Jack said.

"Let's move on," Mason urged.

3. Although Fort Scott is in southeastern Kansas, in the 1840s it was considered to be in Missouri, on the eastern side of the permanent Indian frontier, which ran from Minnesota to Texas. Although it sounds improbable now, the military was charged with keeping settlers from encroaching on Indian lands to the west. This policy lasted only until after the Mexican War, when the size of the United States was roughly doubled by lands ceded by Mexico—and the idea of Manifest Destiny took hold.

"I'll move when I'm ready," Mad Jack said. "You're getting a mite peevish, Mason. Why don't you finish your breakfast and relax a bit?"

Mason slapped the table in disgust.

"I'd best check the horses," he said, then stood wearily. "We're not half an hour ahead of the Federals."

He walked to the front door, still shaking his head, and he had no sooner stepped onto the porch when a rifle shot rang out. He fell in the doorway, a bullet hole in his forehead, his eyes still open.

It was the first time I had seen a man shot, and it both terrified and fascinated me. Mother threw herself on the floor beside me and covered my body with hers, but I managed to peek over her shoulder at the drama that was unfolding.

"I'm ready to move now," Mad Jack said.

He kicked over the table and a revolver appeared in each of his hands. They were much bigger than the one he had consigned to the floor along with the ham and eggs. Then he and the youngest guerrilla huddled beneath the window.

The young one dared a glimpse above the sill.

"How many?" Mad Jack asked.

"A squad," he said. "They've taken our horses."

"Damn."

"What about the back door?"

"That's what they expect," Mad Jack said.

"What about Mason?"

"The back of his head is gone," Mad Jack said. "He's gone to his Maker."

"But we can't leave him like that," the other said. "He was our friend."

The young man crawled over the floor of the cabin, keeping low, and grasped Mason's nearest arm. As he hauled the body back into the cabin, a bloody stain from the back of Mason's head smeared the planks. Then, when the Yankees realized they were being denied the body of the victim, they shot several more times, and the corpse jerked each time from the impact of the balls.

When the young guerrilla had the body fully in, he kicked the front door shut with the toe of his boot. A couple of rifle shots pierced the door at waist level and shattered the dishes in Mother's sideboard along the far wall.

"That's not a squad," Mad Jack said. "It's a whole company."

"Now what do we do?" the young guerrilla asked.

"We make them unload the rest of their guns," Mad Jack said. "Take that chair and prepare to throw it through the window. Then, we make a dash for it."

The young man drew one of the chairs to him.

Mad Jack cocked his revolvers.

"Now," he said.

The chair crashed through the window, showering the porch with frame and glass and Mother's lace curtain. A volley of shots followed, and Mother held tightly to me as the balls zipped through the cabin.

Mad Jack walked to the door, stepped over the body of his fallen friend, and began firing both pistols at the Yankee soldiers, who were hiding behind the woodpile and split-rail fence outside.

"Ha!" he shouted. "Go to hell! It ain't my time yet!"

I could hear the bark of Mad Jack's pistols as he cocked and fired in an unhurried rhythm, and the shouts and clatter of the soldiers as they dove for cover.

Then the young man ran out the door, a pistol in his hand and the tail of his butternut coat flying behind him.

I squirmed a bit in Mother's grasp, and through the window I saw the soldiers as they reloaded, hands flying as they poured powder and ball down the barrels and rammed them home. A pair of troopers emerged from behind a woodpile and gave chase to the young man, who had fled in the direction of the barn.

One of the soldiers carried a Sharp's carbine.

I heard the boom of the carbine and I knew that the young guerrilla was dead.

Then silence descended upon the cabin. Through the window, I could see billows of smoke from the guns drift across the yard in the early morning breeze. There wasn't a sign of Mad Jack.

Then Mason, the guerrilla who had been shot in the head, moaned.

Mother went to him and knelt near his head.

Mason's eyes fluttered strangely and his mouth moved in an attempt to speak.

Mother cradled his bloody head in her lap.

"Don't try to talk," she said.

"Mary," I heard Mason say.

"I'm not Mary."

"Mary, I love you."

A tear rolled down Mother's cheek. "I know, my love."

Mason nodded. "The boys—"

"They are well."

"Thank you," he said. Then his face became serene. His eyes were glazed and his blood was spreading on the floor beneath them. "The sun," he said. "Where has it gone? It is still morning. Where has the sun gone?"

Mother rocked him.

"Darling Mason, it is late," she said. She wiped her tears away with the palm of one hand. "Your work is done. You have come in from the fields, we have had our supper, and now we must talk no more, for it is time to sleep."

"Yes," Mason said drowsily. His breathing was quick and shallow. "I would like that. Will you sing me to sleep?"

Mother shut her eyes and softly began.

"*In Banbridge town / near the County Down / one morning last July,*" she sang, "*down a boreen green / came a sweet colleen / and she smiled as she passed me by. / She's the gem of Ireland's crown, / Young Rosie McCann / from the banks of the Bann, / she's the star of the County Down.*"

His breathing stopped.

# Four

A Union captain stepped through the door, his Remington revolver drawn.

"Don't shoot," Mother said as she rose from the floor. "He's gone. They're all gone."

"Did they hurt you?"

"No," she said. "They just made me cook."

A bandage was slung around the captain's head. There was a bloody spot in the bandage over his right ear, and his neck was caked with dried blood.

"You're lucky," the captain said. "Mad Jack ambushed us two days ago, while we slept, and he had nearly chewed my ear off before my men pulled him off me."

"Why didn't they shoot him then?"

"Because he was unloading his revolvers at them by that time," the captain said sourly. "It was the first time that I had ever been in a skirmish where the preferred weapon was a set of teeth. They were sharp and not particularly clean, and I'll be lucky if gangrene does not set in."

"I've witnessed his hygiene," Mother said.

The captain returned the gun to his flap holster.

"Where's your husband?"

"Gone with Porter," mother said.

"Porter, eh?" the captain said. "Then you'll have to leave."

"Pardon?"

"The cabin must be burned," he said. "You've given comfort to the enemy, and your man has taken up arms against us. Surely you know the General Orders by now. It's martial law in Missouri."

The captain took a folded newspaper from inside his coat and thrust it at Mother. She glanced at it briefly, then thrust it into her apron.

"These insurgents are criminals," the captain said. "They survive with the help of folks like you, who profess during the daylight that they know nothing, but at night feed and shelter them."

"But where are we to go?" she asked.

"You must have some kin nearby."

"No, there is no one."

"Then you can seek comfort with your rebel friends," he said. "Look, there is no time. We are in pursuit of a monster. Can you not see what he did to my ear? He would have chewed the other one off as well had my men not pulled him off me."

The captain looked at the bloodstain on Mother's apron.

"You seem to have been familiar with that one."

"No," she said. "We had never seen these men before. I simply offered human comfort while he died."

"It was more than he deserved," the captain said. Then he bellowed for his sergeant.

"Take this secesh woman and her brat outside," he said. "Then fire the cabin and the outbuildings."

"What about our things?" she asked. "There are books, and family articles, and—"

"There is no time," the officer said.

The sergeant grasped Mother by the arm, but she shook him off.

"I can walk on my own," she said. "Jacob, fetch your coat and scarf. It's cold outside."

I took my things from the rack near the door, and followed Mother outside. We waited a safe distance away in the yard and watched.

The sergeant motioned for two of the soldiers, and they took our lamps from the tables and walls and began to slush coal oil on the walls of the cabin and over the body of the dead guerrilla inside.

Then they took a bundle of kindling from the box near the fireplace, set the sticks alight from the blaze in the hearth, and threw them against the walls of the cabin.

The coal ignited with a sound like that of smartly flapping a blanket.

The soldiers trotted out the front door.

"Father's fiddle," I said.

"No," Mother said, grasping me tightly.

"We can't let it burn," I said, and twisted wildly until I slipped from her grasp. She tried to catch me, but I was too fast.

I held my scarf over my mouth and nose as I entered the burning cabin. I tripped over the body of the dead man and found myself on my hands and knees, between the corpse and the undulating flame that separated me from the old fiddle and bow that hung from a peg on the wall in front of me.

Then I dashed forward, leapt over the flames, snatched the fiddle and bow from the wall, and ran back, jumping the corpse and escaping unscathed through the front door.

Mother caught me on the porch, and dragged me out onto the yard by my suspenders. There we fell to the cold ground on our knees and hugged one another tightly.

Then she slapped me.

"Don't you ever disobey me again," she said.

# Five

The cabin went up like a torch. The soldiers had mounted their horses and left in pursuit of Mad Jack, leaving Mother and me to watch the flames consume our home. When the roof sagged and fell in, I began to sniffle.

"Don't cry," Mother said.

She took a piece of hemp cord she had found and tied one end to the scroll of the fiddle and the other beneath the tailpiece, then secured the bow beneath the fiddle, to make a neat package. Then she slung the cord over my shoulder, so that I could carry the fiddle on my back and have my hands free.

"Aren't you cold?" I asked. She wore no coat, just her apron over a simple plaid skirt and matching bodice.

"Yes," she said.

"Why'd the soldiers do it?" I asked.

"Because they could," she said.

Mother ventured to the side of the cabin, where the dead young guerrilla was sprawled faceup on the ground near the back fence. The round from the Spencer had taken him squarely in the back and exited his chest, and as he fell his head had struck a sharp stone, leaving a bloody gash in his forehead.

"Stay here," Mother said. We were about ten yards away from the body, and I dropped to my knees.

Mother knelt beside the body. She put a finger against the side of his throat, checking for a pulse, and apparently found none. Then she reached behind her and pulled free the string of her apron, which was still bloody from the wounds of the guerrilla whose body had burned in the cabin. She withdrew the newspaper the captain had given her, then wadded the apron into a ball and threw it over the fence into the weeds.

Then she unbuttoned the heavy homespun coat and tried to tug it from the body. She pulled at a sleeve, but the body simply moved along with each effort. Mother brushed the hair from her eyes, put both hands beneath the body, and rolled it over.

With the corpse on its belly, it was easier for Mother to grasp the coat by the sleeves and pull it free. She inspected the coat, brushing the dirt away, and ignoring the traces of blood where the fatal bullet had entered.

She donned the coat, smoothing the rough fabric.

Then she discovered a lump in the right pocket, reached inside, and pulled out a cap-and-ball revolver. The soldiers had taken the gun that the guerrilla had fired at them while trying to escape, but they had missed this one. It was a Manhattan revolver, .36-caliber, and loaded and capped.

Mother ran her finger over the cylinder and then down the barrel. Then she replaced the revolver in the pocket. She folded the newspaper and shoved it beside the gun.

"Come on," she said, extending her hand to me. "We have to go."

She pulled me away.

"But town is the other way," I said.

"We're not going to town," she said. "We're going to Marion County."

# Six

We made our way through the woods with haste until, half an hour later, we emerged at the tracks of the St. Joseph and Hannibal Railway. Mother climbed the grade and stood between the rails, craning her head in both directions.

The tracks went on forever in both directions.

"This way," she said, and began pulling me down the tracks.

But after thirty yards, she stopped, uncertain of the direction she had chosen. We had wound our way around many hills and thickets, down a few draws, and she had lost her sense of direction.

Her face shone with sweat, and in a couple of places briars had drawn blood to her cheeks. She wiped her face with the sleeve of the coat.

"Jacob," she said. "Before the war, when you took the train to St. Louis with your father. Do you remember in which direction the train went?"

I looked in both directions.

"Well?"

"No," I said.

"Damn," she said. "Try to remember."

She wiped her brow again, then in exasperation reached behind her and took the pins that held her hair in the bun. She shook her head and her red hair fell down around her shoulders.

"We should go the other way," I said.

"Why?"

I pointed to the ground.

"Our shadows are in front of us," I said. "It's morning, so that means we're heading west. Father taught me that. We should go in the other direction."

"Good boy," she said.

# Seven

We walked for miles. First we took the middle of the rails, trying to match our steps to the spacing of the ties, and when that proved too tiring, we moved to the side, trying to make our way along the embankment. But walking at an angle soon hurt our ankles and we returned to the tracks, soon finding that we could usually pick a line along the highest spot of the ballast between the ties, which was somewhat more bearable.

Sometimes, to relieve the boredom, I walked *on* the rails, my arms outstretched for balance. But I quickly grew weary of even that and fell in again beside Mother.

Eventually, we came to a rough-hewn blockhouse that guarded a trestle across a river. The door of the blockhouse was open, and smoke billowed from the stovepipe above the shake roof.

Mother slowed, and grasped my hand in hers, but we continued on with measured steps toward the bridge.

We had almost passed the blockhouse when a voice called out.

"Halt!"

A corporal came out of the doorway, buckling a revolver around his waist. The top buttons of his blouse were open, revealing a pair of red underwear, and on his sleeves he wore the chevrons of a corporal. He was older, with a short beard, and his kepi was pushed back on the top of his head.

We stopped, and Mother put a protective arm around my shoulders.

"It's cold and we have business on the other side," Mother said.

"I'm sorry, ma'am," the soldier said. "We have orders to stop all civilians attempting to cross the Salt River."

"Whatever for?" Mother asked. "This is still our bridge and our river, are they not?"

"Your people keep burning your own bridge," the corporal said. "Nobody is allowed across without a military pass. Do you have a pass?"

Mother's face hardened.

"I'm Eliza Gamble," she said. "We are on our way to the prison at Palmyra to visit my husband, John Gamble . . . and it may be the last time the boy sees his father alive."

I looked at Mother in alarm.

The soldier swallowed hard and looked away.

"Is he one of the ten?" he asked.

"I don't know," mother said.

She slipped her hand into the right pocket of the coat, and as I was on her left side, opposite the soldier, I could glimpse the butt of the revolver. She smiled as she removed the newspaper that was tucked there, and the flap of the pocket fell back, hiding the revolver.

She unfolded the paper.

"It says here that the names of the ten to be executed shall be announced today."

She offered the newspaper to the corporal, who took it reluctantly and stared at the black-bordered notice.

"You can't read," Mother said.

"No, ma'am."

She took back the paper.

"It is a letter addressed to Colonel Joseph C. Porter," she said.

Then she cleared her throat and began to read:

"Sir, this is to notify you that the deadline has passed for the safe return of Andrew Allsman to his family and I can only presume his murder. Ten men who have belonged to your band, and unlawfully sworn to by you to carry arms against the government of the United States, will be shot dead on Saturday, the 18th of October, 1862, as a meet reward for this crime. The names of the condemned will be posted the Friday before the execution."

Then she paused and pretended to choke back tears.

"It is signed W. R. Strachan,[1] provost marshal general."

Mother seemed to spit the name from her mouth.

1. Donovan's interview, taken from Gamble's oral account, rendered the name of the provost marshal phonetically, as *Strawn*. The name has been changed to reflect the correct spelling throughout.

I began to cry, and bit my bottom lip in an attempt to stem the flow. I expected her to slap me, or at least chide me for betraying my emotions. Instead, an unexpected—and for me, a not entirely convincing— maternal look crossed her face as she knelt and dabbed at my tears with the hem of her dress.

"Now, Jacob," she said. "We must be brave. Father was taken while doing his duty, and we should behave in a way that would make him proud of us, too."

My tears, of course, did not stop. The corporal was looking more than a little distraught as well.

Mother stood.

"Do your children still breathe, Corporal?"

He looked away.

"Well?"

The corporal awkwardly doffed his kepi and looked at the ground.

"Forgive me, madam," he said. "You may pass."

"Thank you," she said. Then she added with ice: "You are almost too kind to be a Yankee."

And that is how we crossed the Salt.

# Eight

## From Donovan's notes

"Let's leave you and your mother on that bridge for a moment," I said, then took another drink of whiskey. "I'm a bit confused."

"It was quite a bridge," Gamble said. "The water below looked quite cold. But I couldn't help but to stop in the middle to hawk a gob of spit over the side."

"Charming," I said. "But who the hell is Andrew Allsman and this Strachan character? I thought we were going to be talking about Alf Bolin."

"You told me to start at the beginning," Gamble said. "We will get to Bolin, by and by."

"Help me make sense of this."

Gamble sighed.

"Let me explain," he said. "The war had seemed like some kind of great game when it started. There was lots of talk early on about giving the Yankees a whipping, but rarely did a skirmish result in more than a handful of casualties. With prisoners, the custom was to grant a field parole—a scrap of paper that promised the bearer would never again take up arms—and to send them home. The boys would often collect three or four such paroles, carrying the most recent one in their jacket, and continue to slip away to become partisan soldiers."

"Get to the point," I urged.

"When martial law was declared in August of 1861, new orders called for the execution of insurgents on the spot. Men who had been content to fight to a draw and go home were now locked in a battle to the death."

"And Strachan?"

"He was the head of the military police in our corner of the state," he said, and took a cigar from the pocket of his vest. "He was particularly hated because he turned against his neighbors in Shelby County. The provost system was universally corrupt, a license to kill and steal from the federal government, and most folks were more scared of the local provost than of the devil himself."

Gamble stuck the cigar in the corner of his mouth and struck a match on the tabletop.

"I would rather you didn't smoke," I said.

"Men's rules, remember?" he asked, puffing away.

"Fine," I said. "So martial law was declared, partisans were being executed, and the provosts were murderers and thieves."

"Ah, the worst was yet to come," Gamble said. "General Order Nineteen called for all men to report to the nearest Union military post for duty. Thousands of men who previously considered themselves neutral were suddenly forced to choose sides. Father threw in with old Joe Porter because, he said, we Gambles still had plenty of relations in Tennessee and it wouldn't be proper to side against family. Mother, an educated but superstitious woman, was against it. The cards advised caution, she said."

"So your father joined the wrong side."

"Careful," Gamble said. "I remain unreconstructed."

"All right," I said. "He joined the losing side."

"Father didn't even have a uniform, and he carried an old hunting rifle and a belt knife, and he caught up with Porter's army exactly one day before the battle of Auxvasse Creek.[1] There, Porter's command was shot to pieces when Odon Guitar brought his cannon to bear on the irregulars hidden in the timber along the creek. But Porter and a few of his men escaped to the north."

"And Allsman?"

"Andy Allsman was a Yankee informer who had been captured when Porter raided Palmyra in September. Porter held the city for only two hours, but he succeeded in liberating forty-five inmates from the federal prison, capturing some guns and ammunition, and shooting the living hell out of the large copper ball that graced the cupola atop the Marion County Courthouse. He grabbed old Allsman on his way out of town."

"What became of him?"

1. Donovan again uses phonetics, spelling the name of the creek "Ohvah." This is one of the pitfalls of using short-hand, and had her interview with Gamble seen print, a copy editor certainly would have made these corrections before publication.

"It's a mystery," he said. "Some say he was shot by a detail assigned to escort him back to the Federals, and I reckon that was so. But on that particular Friday in October, it was the first time I'd heard the name, and I hated him. I hated Allsman for being a Union sympathizer and hated him because of the influence his kidnapping had had on my family. As terrible as his fate must have been, I reckon he had it coming—after all, the only man in the county who had voted for Abe Lincoln in 1860 was run out of town on a rail. What could a Yankee informer expect?"

# Nine

Around noon we encountered a section of track that had been destroyed by the guerrillas. For a length of a hundred yards or so, the rails had been ripped up and placed over a pyre of railway ties, which had been set on fire. The rails had drooped and twisted from the heat, rendering them useless.

But the ashes were cold and those who had conducted the sabotage were long gone.

We were in a clearing, and far on the opposite side Mother spied a farmhouse that seemed relatively unscathed by the war. Mother took my hand and led me down into a creek bottom, and sat me on a log.

"Jacob, I want you to rest here for a moment."

"Don't leave me."

She patted my knee, in an unconvincing attempt to be comforting.

"I won't be gone but a moment," she said.

"Is it true about Father?"

"Perhaps," she said.

"You could have made it up," I said. "The soldier

couldn't read. You could have made up that whole story about the men to be executed."

"Jacob," she said, "all I know is that ten men who were with Porter are to be executed. I only found out myself this morning, when the Yankee captain handed me the newspaper. I had intended to tell you when the time was right, but the situation at the river demanded that I use the information to its best effect. Your tears were our passage across that bridge."

I began to cry again.

"I despise you," I said.

"You can despise me all you want, but right now, you are to stay put. Whatever happens, you are to remain here. Understood?"

"Yes'um."

She softened a bit.

"If you become frightened, you may play our song," she said.

"The one you sang to the dying man."

"Yes," she said. "You play it on that fiddle and I will come straightaway."

She kissed me on the top of the head and left.

Never had I felt so alone.

I was keen to every sound around me: the rustle of the wind in the trees, the murmur of the stream, and the lonely honking of a flock of geese that passed just above the tops of the trees. High in the sky was a group of turkey buzzards, which wheeled in lazy circles, searching for some dead or dying thing to feed upon.

How much time passed, I cannot say. It may have been fifteen minutes, or it may have been an hour, but eventually the cold soaked into my skin and I grew restless. I thought if I could just walk around a bit, it would restore some warmth to my limbs, so I left the stump and ventured down the creek bed.

It wasn't long before I came to a series of bluffs. I climbed the steep and wooded bank and found myself beneath one of the bluffs, and there I paused at the lip of a shallow cave beneath a massive overhang. I stared at the sky for some time, watching thunderheads creep across the deep blue October sky. It wasn't raining yet, but I knew that it soon would be.

Then I decided to climb higher, over the bluffs, and discovered an old family cemetery that had been located on the plateau there, overlooking the creek bottom. The cemetery was bounded by an old iron fence. I walked through to the gate, which was hanging by a single hinge, and entered the graveyard, which was overgrown with buffalo grass. Time and weather had made the inscriptions on the stones difficult to read, but the latest date I could make out was 1824. Here and there, the monuments were topped with a lonesome stone cross that peeked above the rustling grass.

I found a grassy spot in front of the most impressive monument, unslung the fiddle and bow from my back, and sat down. I held the fiddle in my lap, tested the strings with my thumb, and adjusted the pegs as my father had taught me to bring it into tune.

I was growing increasingly anxious.

I placed the bow upon the strings and played a bit. The tune was "Star of the County Down," the first song that Mother had taught me, and our favorite. It was a simple melody, a sad and slow-moving ballad, and played in the confines of the forgotten graveyard, it was even more melancholy.

Then someone reached from behind me and snatched the bow from my right hand. It nearly scared me out of my wits and I jumped several feet away.

"Hullo, what have we here?" asked a thin man dressed in a long black coat. He had a mustache and hair that brushed the back of his collar, and his clothes were surprisingly clean. Around his neck he wore a cravat, in the center of which was a fancy stickpin.

"Hey!" I said. "That's my father's."

"And what a good daughter you are to watch over it so carefully."

"I'm no girl," I said.

"My mistake," the man said. "But an easy one to make, considering your delicate features and that head of fine blond hair. You see, I've been watching you for quite a spell."

"I thought somebody was."

"I didn't mean to scare you."

"I ain't scared," I lied.

"Of course you're not," the man said. "But as I was saying, I have been watching as you prepared to play, and it struck me that things were a little out of kilter."

"I scarcely got a sound out."

"I've gone by many names," he said, "but you can call me Lucius Nightshade. At your service."

He tipped his head.

"Are you a guerrilla?"

"You could say that."

"You don't look like any guerrilla I've ever seen. You're too clean."

"I'll take that as a compliment," Nightshade said. "Now, as I was saying, it was your technique that caught my eyes. I've played the fiddle for a long while. May I see the instrument?"

"I shouldn't."

"Come now, do you think I would steal your father's amusement? I may be light-fingered, but I'm not petty."

Reluctantly, I handed him the fiddle.

"Did your father teach you to play?"

"No, my mother."

Nightshade shook the fiddle. Something rattled inside, and he brought the fiddle close to his face and peered into one of the holes on either side of the bridge.

"Your father put the rattlesnake buttons inside?"

"He said it makes it sound better."

Nightshade shook his head.

"What is your name . . . boy?"

"Jacob Gamble."

"And tell me, Jacob Gamble, which hand do you use for writing your lessons? What hand does the master strike when you make mistakes?"

I held up my right hand.

Nightshade rapped it smartly with the bow.

"Now, tell me which hand you wanted to write with."

"The other," I said, shaking my smarting fingers.

"Did the schoolmaster make you change?"

"He said the left hand is the devil's hand."

"And I'll bet he said the fiddle is the devil's box

as well," Nightshade said. "What nonsense. Have you ever tried holding the stick in your left hand?"

I shook my head.

"Here," he said. "Try it."

He handed back the fiddle and bow, and I switched hands. I awkwardly drew the horsehair across the strings.

"Feel better?" he asked. "More natural?"

In the distance, there was the sound of baying dogs. I also thought I heard a couple of gunshots.

"What's that sound?" I asked.

"Trouble, I'll bet. Keep playing."

I tried again, and after a few false starts, managed to play a few bars of "County Down," even though I had to adjust because the strings now seemed reversed. Surprisingly, it did feel more natural, but the sound could not have been pleasant to listen to.

"Bravo," he said, clapping. "Well done."

"But it's backwards," I protested.

"You could go all left-handed, you know, by swapping the coarse and the fine strings," he said. "That way the notes would be where you expect them to be."

"Hadn't thought of that."

"I'll bet I could teach you a lot of things you hadn't thought of," he said, and sat down on the grass next to me. "Tell me, my young friend—what are you and your pretty mother doing in the middle of Misery[1] all alone?"

"How do you know about her?"

"I see a great many things," Nightshade said.

"My father needs us."

---

1. Derogatory slang for Missouri.

"What kind of father would leave a family to fend for themselves during a time of war?"

"He's at the prison at Palmyra."

"Why, that's not good at all," Nightshade said, but the tone of his voice implied the opposite. "And what do you and your mother think you can do about it?"

"Save him, of course."

Nightshade shook his head sadly.

"Oh, son," he said. "I'm afraid you'll need more than good intentions. Not even a battery of artillery could break that jail. The cells are made of steel plate, built like an ironclad, and the stone walls are pinned together with cannonballs."[2]

"You're lying."

"I never lie."

"Then what can we do?"

"Things do look grim," Nightshade said. "How long has your mother been gone?"

"I don't know," I said. "Not long."

"Why, I watched you for an hour or more, I reckon," he said. "Don't you think she should be back by now?"

I shrugged.

"She would have returned by now," he said, "if only she could."

"What do you mean by that?"

2. This description of the Marion County Jail, which was used as the federal prison during the Civil War, is true. The jail was built in 1858 and touted as the best built west of the Mississippi. The claim was no exaggeration. The jail and its antebellum cells were in continuous service until 1992, when the county vacated the building. It has since been placed on the National Register of Historic Places.

"Something might have happened to her."

"Like what?"

"Could be just about anything," Nightshade said. "Those dogs we heard may have torn her to pieces, or she could have gotten shot or knifed or strangled, or . . ."

"Or what?" I demanded.

"She could simply have left you," he said. "Some mothers do. A child can be an awful burden, especially when you're about to become a widow."

I wiped a tear from my eye with my cuff.

"Perhaps you had better come with me."

"No," I said. "She told me to wait."

"And wait you have," Nightshade said. "You may still be waiting at midnight. How would you like to be in the woods all alone in the dark?"

"I ain't afraid," I said. "I'll wait."

"You are afraid of the dark, aren't you?" Nightshade asked. "But that's brave talk. Seems to me you're badly in need of a boon companion. Tell me, have you any money?"

Nightshade moved closer.

"Wouldn't tell if I did," I said.

"Secrets make the world go round," he said.

Nightshade touched my scarf. He moved it aside, then slid his fingers under my collar and to the back of my neck. Then he leaned close and whispered in my ear.

"Your mother might not love you anymore," he said. "She might love your father enough to make a deal when she gets to Palmyra—and you'd just be in the way. She's young, isn't she? Even if your father is dead, she will search for someone to take

his place. You'll know that you have been replaced
in her affections when she asks you to stop calling
her Mother, and asks to be called by her first name,
as a brother might call an older sister."

"You're a damn liar," I shouted.

"I'm cursed to tell the truth," Nightshade said,
"even when lies would be ever more pleasant."

"That's enough," Mother said from the cemetery
gate. In one hand she held the Manhattan and in the
other was a cloth sack. Her hair was rippling in the
breeze and her blue eyes shone with determination.

"Mother Gamble has returned," Nightshade said
casually. "Out stealing food, are we?"

"Get away from him," she said.

She walked through the grass to within a few
steps, threw me the sack, and held the revolver in
both hands, pointing at Nightshade's chest.

"I'm sitting awfully close," he said. "Aren't you
afraid of shooting your own child?"

Mother stepped closer, dropped to her knees,
and placed the muzzle against the back of Nightshade's neck.

"Not now," she said.

Nightshade laughed as I scooted away with the
sack of food.

"I could help you," Nightshade said easily, glancing over his shoulder at Mother. "I know the provost
marshal. We're on speaking terms, you might say.
It could be to your advantage. We could make a
deal. We could make many deals."

"*Apage Satanas*," mother said.

Nightshade disappeared. It wasn't in a puff of
smoke exactly, and he may have left while I was

rummaging in the sack for a hunk of bread, but when I looked up, he was gone.

"Come," Mother said, taking my hand. "Let's put some ground between us and this awful place."

# Ten

That knowledge that Mother had stolen food, possibly at the point of a gun, to provide for me made me forget some of the things that Nightshade had said. I have eaten many fine meals in my life, but I have remembered none as well as the lunch of pork and bread that Mother brought in that flour sack.

It began to rain when we reached the tracks, but we continued walking. And it seemed we followed those rails to the east forever, through silent woods, creek bottoms, and fields that had gone untended since the war broke out. I had never walked so far in one day in my life, and my wet shoes and damp clothes made the trek all the more miserable.

By and by, the rain stopped and the sun sank low in the west, and we were following our shadows once more. A locomotive appeared on the eastern horizon, belching smoke from its stack, and as it neared, Mother pulled me safely to the side of the tracks.

Behind the locomotive were a half-dozen flatcars,

loaded with rails and ties to repair the broken section we had passed that morning. Soldiers were also sitting on the flatcars, rifles held across their knees, and as they passed they jeered and hooted. Some shouted obscenities, and others made suggestive gestures at Mother.

She watched the train pass without expression.

When it was gone, we climbed back onto the tracks and continued our journey. The polished rails gleamed like fire from the slanting rays of the sun.

We arrived at Palmyra as the sun was setting, and from the tracks we took Main Street and followed it into town proper. We reached the courthouse square a few blocks on, and Mother knew the way to the jail, which was just a block or so away, on the corner of Dickerson and Lafayette Streets.

The building seemed huge.

Up front was a two-story brick office building, in Greek Revival style, and behind it stretched the fortresslike stone walls of the jail. A Union encampment occupied the yard in front, and there was all the activity one would expect of soldiers at twilight—joking, playing cards, cooking. A couple of cannons and their limbers stood menacingly between us and the jail.

Before we advanced, Mother knelt and wiped the road dirt from my cheeks.

"This is very serious, Jacob," she said. "It's important that you keep still no matter what happens. A word from you at the wrong time might ruin our chances. So you are to keep silent, even though you may hear some things that upset you or which you know are lies."

We stepped forward and, near the entrance to the jail office, encountered a rotund sergeant with a pair of glasses perched on his nose. He was sitting on a camp stool and, by the light of a candle lantern, was whittling one of those silly wooden chains that idle folks are so fond of. From a staff above him hung the Union flag with thirty-four stars.

"Begging your pardon," Mother said. "Have the names of the ten been posted?"

"Yes, ma'am."

The sergeant pointed with the knife to a notice that had been nailed to a post. Mother went to it, but it was too dark now for her to read it. She removed the paper from the nail and carried it into the circle of light cast by the sergeant's lantern. When she replaced the notice on the post, her hands were trembling.

She waited for a moment, but the sergeant was absorbed in his whittling and did not look up.

"Pardon," she said.

"Yes?"

"I have traveled some distance and desire a word with the provost marshal," Mother said gently.

"Provost Marshal General Strachan is not available," the sergeant said. "Come back tomorrow, madam."

"Tomorrow will be too late," she said. "I really must speak with him this evening. It is of some importance."

"There's nothing I can do," the sergeant said, running a hand over the half-finished wooden chain. "Come back tomorrow."

Mother squared her shoulders and lifted her chin.

"Sergeant, you don't understand," she said. "My son and I have walked all the way from our farm in Shelby County. We must be allowed an audience with the provost marshal."

"I apologize, madam," the soldier said. "But that is impossible. I am the chief jailer, so am in a position to know. Better that you come back tomorrow."

"Now, see here," Mother said, her voice rising. "My husband is scheduled to be shot tomorrow and I must speak with Provost Marshal General Strachan."

The man looked at her with eyes devoid of pity.

"There has been some terrible mistake," Mother said. She was shouting now. "I will set things right."

The sergeant shook his head.

Mother stood there, her chest heaving and her hand clenched.

A middle-aged man in a uniform lacking insignia of any kind walked to the edge of the porch, which was lit by a couple of oil lanterns. The man had long dark hair and a carefully trimmed beard, and he was wreathed in the smoke from a cigar he held to his lips.

The sergeant dropped his whittling and stood at attention.

The man with the cigar eyed Mother carefully before speaking.

"What's the trouble here?"

"Sir," the sergeant said. "This female demands an audience. She says her husband is one of the ten."

"Is that so?" the man asked.

He gestured with the cigar.

"Come closer, madam, into the light."

Mother smoothed the homespun coat and stepped

forward, extending her hand palm-down. The man clutched it in his fist and peered intently at her.

"I believe I know this woman," he said. "It has been some years, but you are Elizabeth Dunbar, are you not?"

"Why, yes, I am," she said. "Or rather, I was. Dunbar is my maiden name. I believe my father was your comrade in Willock's Battalion during the Mexican campaign."

The sergeant and I exchanged surprised looks.

Strachan kissed her hand.

"Why not step inside, out of the cold?" Strachan suggested.

*unslung*

# Eleven

Strachan opened the door to his office. Inside, a table was laden with food. Candles flickered. There was a potbellied stove on the far side of the room, and the temperature was so warm as to be uncomfortable.

"Sit there," Strachan told me, indicating a seat at the table.

I unslung the fiddle, placed it beside the chair, and sat quietly while Strachan walked to his desk in the far corner. On the wall behind him was a map of the Trans-Mississippi West. He waited until Mother had taken the chair in front of the desk, then lowered himself into a leather chair.

"Perhaps you would care to partake," Strachan said, and indicated the table of food.

"I couldn't," Mother said, "but I reckon Jacob might. You know how boys are."

Strachan motioned his approval.

I glanced at Mother, who nodded. As I filled a plate with fried chicken and ham, Strachan pro-

Shoved
Wiped

duced a bottle of brandy and filled a pair of glasses
on his desk.

"May I take your coat?" Strachan asked.

"How kind," she said. "But I believe I am still
chilled from the night."

"This will warm you."

Strachan shoved the glass of brandy toward her.

"Which one of the ten is yours?" he asked.

Mother took the glass, drained it, and wiped her
mouth with the back of her hand.

"My husband is John Gamble," she said. "He is a
good man."

"A number of good men have died in this war,"
Strachan said as he refilled her glass. "Go on."

"I'm certain there has been some mistake," she
said. "John Gamble is not really a soldier. He's a
farmer. That's all he's known."

"But he was captured with Porter's men at Auxvasse Creek," Strachan said. "And he is a Southern
sympathizer. Our intelligence in that regard is very
precise. He has apparently been up to more than
corn and cane lately."

"Why wasn't he freed with the others during
Porter's raid?"

"He was too ill to be moved," Strachan said.
"They left him behind so that he could receive care.
His wound, I'm afraid, was quite severe. His leg, I
believe."

"Did he receive care?" mother asked.

"In the measure that he deserved," Strachan said.

Mother drank more brandy.

"My husband is a Peace Democrat," she said.

"Then why did he throw in with Porter?"

"He felt he had no choice."

Strachan puffed on his cigar and drummed his fingers on the desk. She finished the second glass of brandy and asked for another.

"Are you not warm yet?" he asked.

"I am approaching that condition," she said.

Strachan leaned forward and made a tent of his long fingers.

"Mrs. Gamble, I don't believe that your problem is insoluble," he said. "There are a number of ways we might go about this. Perhaps what is called for here is . . . a private audience."

Mother forced a smile.

"That might indeed be the thing," she said. Her face was smudged with dirt from the road. Strachan produced a kerchief and handed it to her.

"You may want to—"

"Oh, my face," Mother said. "Goodness. I apologize."

Strachan glanced impatiently at me, then filled Mother's glass once more.

"Before sequestering ourselves," Mother said, dabbing at her face with the kerchief, "I would of course need some manner of assurance that my problem can indeed be resolved."

She folded the kerchief and placed it on the desk.

"It needn't be anything elaborate, you understand," she said. "A written order specifying my husband's release would be sufficient."

"Release?" Strachan asked. "I believe we were bargaining for a stay of execution."

"It is my understanding that John Gamble is severely wounded," she said. "He needs proper care.

demise

To keep him in prison would merely postpone his demise. A full parole is needed."

Strachan sighed.

"You ask for quite a lot," he said.

"Think of what you are asking of me," she said, again growing angry. The fingers of her right hand traced the flap over the pocket of her coat. "A woman's virtue is no cheap thing. Most folks say it is better to be dead than to surrender it. But I say to live without the one you love is a kind of death, and I give myself to you willingly—*willingly, you understand*—in exchange for the release of my husband."

Strachan was silent.

"Do we have a bargain, Marshal Strachan?"

Then Mother stood.

Strachan mistook it as a gesture that she would leave, but I knew she intended something else—her hand was now in the right pocket of the coat, gripping the Manhattan revolver there.

"Sit down," Strachan said. "We have a deal."

She sat down, and her hand emerged empty from the coat pocket.

"I am reluctant to put anything so delicate in writing," Strachan said. "There might be questions of an embarrassing nature from command at St. Louis. I prefer to give the order in person."

"Again, I ask you to consider the delicacy of the thing I surrender," she said. "I must have some assurances before this . . . private audience. Speak the order, if you must, but speak it now."

"And what assurance do I have that you will keep the bargain?"

"You have the word of a woman who loves her

husband," she said. "I will keep the bargain. Give the order."

"This audience," Strachan said. "It will be of some length?"

"Give the order."

Strachan grunted his satisfaction.

"Sergeant McCoy!"

There were footsteps accompanied by muttering, and then the whittling chief jailer we had met outside appeared in the doorway.

"This woman's husband is to be released to her," Strachan said. "She will call for him later tonight. Replace him on the list with . . . oh, what is the name? Smith. Hiram Smith."

"Another replacement?" McCoy asked. "I thought that after the Humphrey woman—"

"Enough, Sergeant," Strachan said. "Those are my orders."

"Yes, sir," McCoy said.

"Dismissed."

"Yes, sir," McCoy said. He saluted, turned on his heel, and left.

"Satisfied?" Strachan asked.

"Quite," Mother said.

Then he turned to me.

"Aren't you finished yet?"

I nodded and pushed the plate away.

"It's all right, Jacob," mother said. "You wait outside and I will be along directly."

I picked up the fiddle and walked for the door. Glancing back as I closed the door behind me, I saw Mother stand and slip the coat from her shoulders before folding it and placing it carefully over her chair.

*Clasped*

# Twelve

I walked out onto the porch. The night had turned colder, and I clasped my coat tight around me. I walked to the edge of the porch and surveyed the Yankee camp, which was now quiet. I noticed that boxes had been stacked in the yard since we had arrived.

I retreated back onto the porch and found a wooden bench. I sat down, placing the fiddle beside me. I was so tired that my arms and legs felt leaden, and I rested my head on the brick wall behind me. I was puzzled by the bargain my mother had made with Strachan, and what might be taking place inside. Even though I was twelve, and knew of sexual relations between men and women, I was still naïve and could not imagine my mother in the embrace of any man save my father.

Sleep had nearly claimed me when the truth bubbled up in my mind. The thought repulsed me, and I marshaled any number of mental arguments against it. Mother had gold on her person, I told myself, and that's what she was trading. But hadn't she used the word *virtue?* That word could not have meant money. Surely it could mean only one thing.

One of the windows of Strachan's office faced the porch.

I got up from the bench and crept over to the window. Most of the candles in the room had been extinguished, but a lamp on the desk still burned.

Strachan still sat in his leather chair, and Mother stood before him. She had removed her dress and undergarments, and her pale skin shone in the warm light cast by the lamp. Then Strachan stood. He brushed her hair from her face. When he placed his arm around her waist and pulled her to him, I covered my mouth and turned away from window.

I stumbled from the porch and fell among the bushes, heaving.

Everything I had eaten that day came up, explosively. The spasms were so violent that it created a stabbing pain in my groin, and the pain terrified me. I thought something had burst inside of me. Pardon me, but to be clear, I did not experience that kind of pain again until being kicked in the balls during a fight some years later.

Finally, when there was nothing left to vomit, I lifted my head and wiped my mouth with my sleeve. My gaze fell upon the boxes in the yard, and I realized that they were newly made pine coffins.

# Thirteen

Mother woke me some time later.

I left the bench and followed her back into the jail, down a hallway past Strachan's closed door, and to an iron hatch that was the entrance to the jail.

Mother rapped on the metal, and a little door in the hatch slammed open. Behind it, we could see the round face of the chief jailer.

"You here for your man?" he asked.

She nodded, and McCoy unlocked the door and swung it open. He was holding an oil lamp in one hand. Once we were inside, he swung the door shut, and it struck home with a sound that reverberated like thunder.

"This way," he said, and led us down a set of iron steps.

Before we had gone twenty feet, we were forced to move to one side of the narrow stairwell to allow passage of a pair of soldiers. Slung between them was a skeletal corpse that was missing his right leg beneath the knee.

As they passed, my mother placed her hand upon my shoulder. Suddenly, her grip became viselike. I squirmed and glanced at Mother's face.

Her eyes were wide in recognition.

The realization finally struck me that the dead man being carried out of the prison was my father. It was the final blow to my senses. No words can describe the dazed and unfeeling place where my mind retreated. I looked at Mother and opened my mouth, but was unable to speak.

She placed a forefinger to her lips.

When the men carrying the body of my father had passed, the jailer continued.

Mother pulled me along behind her.

The jailer led us down another passage, turned a corner, and entered a corridor that smelled of sweat and tobacco smoke. There were a set of high windows in the wall behind us, and the moonlight streamed down, illuminating the tobacco and candle smoke that drifted in layers.

The corridor faced a row of cells. The bars of the cells weren't round, as you might imagine from seeing modern jails, but flat, woven into a lattice, and fastened together with heavy rivets.

The jailer stopped before one of the cell doors.

"The condemned are all in here," he said. "Which one is your husband?"

Some of the men inside were sleeping. Others stood, talking quietly and watching. A tall man just beyond the door was calmly smoking a pipe.

"I don't see him," Mother said. "It is terribly dark, and I don't want to call out for fear of waking the men who are sleeping. May I borrow your lamp?"

McCoy handed her the light, then pulled a short-barreled revolver and held it with one hand while he unlocked the cell door with the other. He stood outside with gun drawn while Mother and I walked inside.

With her back toward the jailer, Mother moved through the cell, examining the face of each man. When she reached the end far end of the cell, she encountered a fat man with wild gray hair and a full beard who was chained by the waist and arms to the latticework.

It was Mad Jack.

Mother leaned close to him and brought up the lamp, so that he could see her face.

"It's your time," she whispered.

Mad Jack lunged at her, snapping his wicked teeth. Then he roared with insane laughter.

"Steer clear of that one," the jailer called.

Mother moved on, moving the lamp from man to man. They ranged from boys to old men and, while they knew they were going to die in the morning, none uttered a single word of lament.

One of the men was about Mother's age. He was the handsomest of the lot, and appeared to be the healthiest. He wore a long coat with a cape over the shoulders, and a hunting shirt embroidered with silk rosettes beneath. When she brought the lamp close, his eyes met hers.

Then he started to ask a question.

Mother placed a hand over his mouth and called over her shoulder, "I have found him!"

She embraced the surprised man.

"Not a word," she whispered as she nestled her head against his shoulder. "But remember, you're injured." Then she put her arm around him and pretended to help him toward the door.

"Stu Akers is your husband?" the jailer asked.

"Of course," Mother said. "Jacob, get on the other side of your father."

With the man between us, we exited the cell.

McCoy slammed and locked the door behind us.

As he led us back down the corridor, I glanced behind me at the cell where the condemned men were held. In the moonlight, I could see that the tall man who was smoking a pipe was leaning through the lattice, watching us recede.

He smiled and gave me a cheerful salute.

I waved back.

"Huzzah!" the man said. "Let's play them out, boys!"

Then a mournful harmonica began to play, and I immediately recognized the ballad as "Lorena." From elsewhere in the prison a fiddle joined in. Then the condemned began to sing, but only the last verse.

*"It matters little now, Lorena, / the past is in eternal past, / our heads will soon lie down,"* they sang in harmony. *"Life's tide is ebbing out so fast, / but there is a future, oh, thank God. / 'Tis dust to dust beneath the sod; / but there, away up there, / 'tis heart to heart."*

The jailer paused.

"We'll have no more of that," he shouted down the corridor.

The music stopped.

But before we had taken three more steps toward freedom, the fiddle struck a new tune, and the entire prison joined it.

*"Oh, I wish I was in the land of cotton, / cinnamon*

*seed, and sandy bottom—* / *look away, look away, look away, Dixie Land!"*

"I will shoot the next man who sings another chorus!" McCoy screamed into the darkness.

*"Oh, in Dixie Land where I was born in . . ."*

The jailer shook his head and continued.

"Damn fools," he muttered. "They don't have the sense God gave geese. If they wake the marshal, he's likely to have them all executed on the spot."

"I doubt if the Provost Marshal General Strachan can hear them," Mother said. "He was sleeping quite soundly when last I saw him."

# Fourteen

We made our way out of the jail and into the night, Stu Akers sagging between us, when it occurred to me that I had left the fiddle and the bow on the porch.

"We have to go back," I said. "Pa's fiddle."

"We mustn't go back," Mother said. "He doesn't need it now anyway."

"But I do," I said bitterly.

We had almost reached the street when the jailer called after us.

"Wait," McCoy said.

We came to a stop. Mother slipped her free hand into her coat pocket, brought out the revolver, and held it tightly against her stomach as the jailer approached from behind.

"I know that ain't your husband," McCoy said, advancing.

Mother thumbed the hammer back. The cylinder turned and locked into place.

Then the jailer stopped, some ten feet behind.

"Stu Akers doesn't have a wife," McCoy said. "I

know because his sister told me so when she inquired today about claiming his body in the morning. She also said Stu is quite the rake, and more than one girl in Hannibal will give a cry when he dies tomorrow."

Mother waited for what would come next.

"If either of you have any regard for your immortal souls—or for the welfare of your poor little bastard—then you had best find a preacher and make things right."

Mother sighed heavily. She eased down the hammer of the Manhattan and then handed the gun to Akers, who slipped it into his waistband.

"Son," the jailer called, "you left your fiddle."

I slipped from beneath Akers's arm, dashed back, and snatched the fiddle from the jailer's hand. I looped it over my shoulder and returned.

The jailer returned inside.

"I don't understand," Akers said in a low voice. "Why me?"

"Because I could," Mother said.

Akers asked where we were taking him, and Mother said the question instead was where he was taking *us*.

"Anywhere but here," Akers said.

"What about Hannibal?" Mother asked. "The fat Yankee said you had family there. A sister?"

"I have no sister," Akers said. "Just a jilted lover seeking the last word. I am from the Ozarks, far in the southwestern corner of the state. We would be safer there, away from this Yankee scourge."

We took the road that led south out of town, never to return to the farm in Shelby County. Of course there was really nothing left to go back to. I had lost my home, I had lost my father, and I had nearly lost my soul.

When I finally started to cry, there seemed no end to the tears. I was sorry for all of it, for my mother and my dead father and for the ten men who, in the morning, would sit on their own coffins in front of a firing squad.

Hell, I was even sorry for the Yankee informer Andy Allsman, and for everyone else who had died so far in that miserable war. About the only person I wasn't sorry for was Strachan. And as my hatred grew, the only thing I could imagine was that Manhattan revolver filling *my* hand.[1]

1. Although there is no record of either John Gamble or Stu Akers among the official records of the Palmyra Massacre, that is not proof that Gamble's account is a lie. Because John Gamble was ordered released, but was already dead, and because Akers was taken by Eliza Gamble in his place, Strachan may have altered the records to deflect suspicion. In 1864, however, Strachan was tried in St. Louis for accepting $500 and sexual favors from the wife of Tom Humphrey in exchange for Humphrey's freedom. Although sentenced to prison, Strachan was released by General Rosecrans on the grounds that the provost had been unjustly prosecuted. Strachan's punishment ultimately amounted to a fine of one dollar.

# Fifteen

Gamble had fallen silent, lost in the past.

"How long did it take you to reach the Ozarks?" I asked, hoping to keep the conversation going.

"The better part of a month during the coldest winter in memory," Gamble said. "It took us ten days to reach the Missouri River, which we crossed by ferry, and then we headed south toward Rolla. Sometimes we made twenty miles a day, and others only five or six. There were a lot of folks on the move, driven from their homes by one side or the other, and we blended in. Akers could have never made it by himself, because the Federals would have assumed correctly that a lone man was a guerrilla who had been driven to seek more hospitable territory. But we appeared to all concerned as a family, and as such we passed relatively easily through the lines."

"What did you eat?"

"What we could beg, or steal," Gamble said. "As we made our way through the wilderness, we used the Manhattan to take small game. Akers showed me how to load and shoot the revolver, and I soon became adept at bagging rabbits and squirrels. There were times when we also took a deer or two, but those were rare, since the gun did not have the range or power of a rifle."

"Where did you get the powder and shot?" I asked.

"We met guerrillas on the trail," Gamble said. "Even if Akers did not know them, he could exchange a few secret words and they would spare us the ammunition, and sometimes a little food. We also asked for horses, but that was one thing they could not afford to share. Often they asked Akers to join them, but he always refused. It was from a sense of obligation, I suppose."

Gamble swirled the whiskey in his glass.

"We didn't expect to be in exile forever," he said. "The South was still winning the war in the East at that time, even though Missouri was lost."

"Why lost?"

"Because of the Battle of Elkhorn Tavern, the previous March. None of the foolish heroics displayed later by Price or Shelby to take back Missouri could alter that fact."

"Elkhorn Tavern?" I asked.

"You're not from here, are you?" Gamble asked. "The Yankees called it Pea Ridge, and it's in northwest Arkansas. Had the Yankees not won, the South would have swept into Missouri and forced the Federals back across the Mississippi River. But Missouri remained broken and bleeding under Federal occupation for the remainder of the war and some years after."

"You must have been in mental anguish, considering the events at Palmyra," I said, tapping my pencil on the tabletop as I formulated the next question.

Gamble smiled.

"I was not in anguish," he said. "That came later. My hatred for Strachan actually sustained me, because it focused my will. The rest of the time, I was too occupied with the activities required for survival to think of much else."

"What stands out in your mind as the worst part of the journey?"

"Truly?"

"Of course."

Gamble uttered the verb form of a common four-letter word.

"Pardon?"

"You heard me," he said. "Elimination."

"It's not a topic I'm used to discussing."

"Defecating in the woods is not a pleasant experience unless you are well prepared," Gamble said. "We were eating food that bordered on the rancid and drinking water that was often unclean. It made all of us sick. Paper was in short supply, we were constantly on the move, and I'm sure your imagination can fill in the rest."

"Dysentery killed more soldiers during the Civil War than bullets," I said, referring to something I had read.

"Makes war seem rather less glorious, doesn't it?" Gamble asked. "I assume that won't make it into your account."

"I'll let the editors worry about it," I said. "But no, it probably won't. Newspapers are always boasting about bringing readers the truth, but they draw the line at anything likely to upset their breakfasts. It tends to diminish newsstand sales and encourage passionate letters about the moral decline of civilization."

"I have always prized daily newspapers," Gamble said, "at times when the Sears and Roebuck was unavailable."

"Indoor plumbing must have seemed a godsend."

The bar was bustling now with the evening trade. The waiter appeared, took our empty glasses from the table, and asked if we cared to order any food.

"Sandwiches would be fine," I said.

"I prefer steak," Gamble said.

"You are costing me a week's pay," I protested.

"Perhaps," Gamble said, "but you are getting a life's story."

"Make that two steaks," I said. "Porterhouses, with the trimmings."

"And how would you like your steaks?" the waiter asked.

"Well done," I said.

"Make mine bloody," Gamble said. "The whiskey in my gut will do the rest."

The waiter turned, but I stopped him.

"Could you bring some writing paper?" I asked. "I'm afraid I've nearly exhausted my supply."

"I'm not sure that we have any stationery, miss."

"Nothing fancy," I said. "Any kind of blank sheets will do."

"I'll see what I can find," he said.

Gamble watched as the waiter retreated.

"You said earlier that you were an unreconstructed rebel," I said.

"What of it?"

"Well, I can't help but wonder your stand on race."

"That seems irrelevant."

"Did your family own slaves?"

"We were poor," Gamble said. "Few people in Missouri did own slaves, except for those involved in the growing of crops that made it economical. It seems beyond reason that preserving the peculiar institution was a rallying cry in Missouri, but most folks had migrated from states where it was considered a way of life. And the preachers constantly reminded us that the God approved of slavery, since so many Bible passages refer to it."

"You seem defensive."

"Slavery is an absolute evil," Gamble said. "No amount of equivocation from pulpit or stump could change that. But the preachers and the politicians would argue still that the earth is flat, if it advanced their political agenda."

"Now you sound like an abolitionist."

"Let me be clear," Gamble said. "We gave no thought to slavery. For us, the war was about survival. I have never judged a human being by skin color, but by action. My hate was reserved for those of my own race who had burned my home to the ground."

He slammed his fist on the table, and the report drew curious looks from other patrons.

"Calm down," I said.

"Don't lecture me," he said. "I am too old for such foolishness."

The waiter returned, carrying a bundle of paper.

"From the stationer next door," he said.

"Very kind," I said.

"Yes, miss," he said. "I will place it on your tab."

The waiter glanced over at Gamble, who was still angry, and then back at me.

"Is everything all right, miss?"

"Of course," I said. "Just a lively debate."

"If you're sure, miss," he said, then backed away.

"Poor bastard," Gamble said.

"Now what's the matter?" I asked.

"That Irishman," Gamble said. "Seems decent enough. Had the sand to ask if you were all right. Probably has a wife and a brood of kids at home to feed. And has to put up with drunks like me in order to do it."

"At least he's working," I said.

"Work is overrated," Gamble said.

"What, you've never worked?"

"I've labored plenty in my life, but I've never worked for a wage," he said. "You're just putting money in somebody else's pocket. Always seemed a poor bargain."

"I have prided myself in honest work," I said.

"Honest work is shoveling coal," he said. "Picking cotton. Going down in the mines with a dinner pail and a carbide lamp. What you do is amusement, except you get paid for it. How does your husband feel about your hobby?"

"My life is not the topic."

"Not married, then," Gamble said.

"I like to think I'm married to my job."

"If it comforts you," he said.

"Well, what of you?" I asked. "Do you have a wife?"

"Several," he said. "They lay in the ground between here and Arizona, all dead before their time—one of pneumonia, two during childbirth, and one of the Spanish influenza. Another killed herself. I like to think that it wasn't my fault, but I'm just lying to myself."

"Why do you say that?"

"She used my gun."

"I'm sorry," I said, a bit flustered. "Let's get back to the Civil War and your story—oh, *damn.*"

"What is it?"

"I have to ask," I said. "Why did she kill herself?"

"She had been told by the county sheriff that I had been killed during a bank robbery at Port Arthur, Texas. It was a mistake—one of my comrades had been killed instead—but before she could be told the truth, she blew her brains out."

I could think of nothing to say.

"Her name was Leigh and she was twenty-six, and beautiful, and I loved her very much—as I did all of them," he said. "Oh, come, don't feel badly for me, it was a long time ago."

"She was twenty-six?"

"Most of my wives were about that," he said, "at least when we married."

"Wasn't that the age of your mother during this story?"

"What of it?"

"Nothing, just—"

"You can't be much more than that," he said.

"No," I admitted. "Not much at all."

I put down my pencil.

"Please, you're old enough to be my great-grandfather."

"You brought it up," he said.

"Let's move on," I said, taking up the pencil

again. "This journey you describe across Missouri. It must have been terribly hard on you."

"I grew leaner, but stronger," Gamble said. "Youngsters are remarkably resilient in that way. But it was much more difficult on my mother. She was a strong woman, but she carried a terrible burden. She seemed to grow more tired every day, but we could not afford to slow our pace. We knew that we would not survive the winter in the wilderness, and had to reach the shelter of the Ozarks by the first snow."

# Sixteen

The snow began to fall just as we left Rolla. The flakes began to swirl from a sky that had turned to pewter, and as we trudged along the road that led to Marshfield, our hopes fell. We were still 150 miles away from Taney County, where Akers said his family would be waiting to welcome us, and we were so weak with exhaustion and lack of food that it didn't seem we could make another 150 yards.

It was mid-morning, as I recall, and Mother simply stopped.

She found a log by the side of the road, sat down, and watched the snow as it dusted the field around us.

"Come on," Akers said. "We can't stop here."

"It seems as good a place as any," she said. "I was hoping for some little charity at Rolla—a bit of food, an offer of a ride with one of the teamsters on their way west, but there was nothing. I should have expected nothing better from a town overrun by Yankees."

"Get up," Akers said. "You sit there and you'll freeze."

"You know we can't walk any longer," she said. "We don't have the food, we don't have the clothing, and we are going to end up as skeletons in a ditch alongside the road."

Akers stared at her.

"What do you propose we do?" he asked with growing anger.

Since she had saved him at the prison at Palmyra, he had been polite and even deferential to her. I had despised him at first because he had taken the place of my father, but as the days had passed, I had come to tolerate and even like him a bit. He wasn't the brightest candle in the tree, but he had never abandoned us, either, even though he had had plenty of chances.

"If you did not have a woman and child in tow," she said, "you would have been home by now, or off with your friends in the brush playing soldier."

"Stop talking nonsense," he said.

"If I were a man, I know what I would do," Mother said.

Akers rubbed the back of his dirty neck.

"How many shots are left in the revolver?" she asked.

"Two," he said. "But this is not a good place to hunt."

"Not if you're hunting animals," Mother said.

"This is not a good place for that, either," Akers said. "I've had some experience in that line of work, and this area is too open and too frequented by the Union supply trains. In no time at all, we would become the hunted."

"At least it would relieve the tedium," Mother said.

"You don't know what you're talking about," Akers said. "The thing you suggest is not as easy as it sounds. It never goes as planned and things get ugly right quick."

"Things are fairly ugly for us," she said.

"Let's go back to Rolla," Akers suggested. "We can find a doorway or a porch to wait out the storm. If worse came to worst, we could throw ourselves on the charity of some church."

"The only charity you'll find there is the stockade," Mother said. "You have no papers, remember? If we linger, some soldier is eventually going to ask to see your pass from whoever the bloody provost marshal is here, and then you're done. But perhaps it would be better than freezing to death in the snow. You go back if you like, but I'm staying here."

"We're not staying here," Akers said. "Eliza Gamble, you are the most stubborn woman that God ever created. I have kept my tongue until now, but if we are to survive this, you are going to get up off your pretty arse and keep walking."

"Don't call me pretty."

Akers clenched his hands and screamed.

"What is wrong with you?" he shouted.

"How can you ask that?" she screamed back at him. "I've lost my home and my husband and I've walked halfway across Missouri and I'm sick. All of us are sick. The boy is running a fever, and if we don't do something now, we're all dead."

"Somebody's coming," I said.

It was snowing harder now, which made it harder

to see, but we could hear a wagon rolling toward us from the west.

"Give me the gun," Mother said.

"No," Akers said. "You'll get yourself killed."

"There's no time to argue," she said.

"Why?"

"Because I have a plan, you cretin," she said.

He handed her the revolver and she slipped it into the pocket of her coat. Then she told Akers and me to throw ourselves in the snow, as if we had been shot and left for dead.

"What's going on?" I asked.

"Hush," Akers said. "Do as your mother says. Fall on the ground and do not get up until we tell you that it is safe."

I did as I was told, but placed my head on my arm so that I could keep one eye on the road.

Mother knelt before us and waited.

As the wagon drew within a hundred yards or so, I could see that it was pulled by a team of mules. There were two men on the seat, but they didn't look like soldiers.

"Close your eyes," mother said.

Then she began to cry softly. She kept her back to the wagon as it drew abreast and finally stopped.

"What's the trouble?" I could hear the driver ask.

Mother didn't answer.

"Madam, can you hear me?" he repeated. "Are those your kin before you?"

"Yes," she said. "We were ambushed."

"It's a good road for that," the driver said.

I opened one of my eyes a bit.

The partner began to climb down from the seat

of the wagon, a shotgun in the crook of his arm, but the driver stopped him.

"This ain't our business," the driver said. "We don't know these people. They could all be bushwhackers."

The driver spat tobacco into the snow.

"But the man and the child are hurt," the partner argued. "We might be able to help them. Rolla is not far away, and we could get them to a doctor there."

The driver spat tobacco into the snow.

Then Mother turned to them, brushing the hair from her face. Her eyes were raw from sickness, but it appeared as if she had been crying.

"You can't help them," she said. "They are both dead, killed for our team and wagon. They are safe with the Lord now, far from this world of trouble, and I am alone."

"Climb up," the mule skinner's partner said. "We'll take you into town."

"Thank you for stopping," Mother said, "but I will not leave their bodies. I cannot bear the thought of the dogs getting to them before they are buried."

"We can't bury your dead," the driver said. "The ground's too hard and we're on a schedule. We've got a load of supplies for the Union army. They can't fight worth a damn, but they sure as hell can eat."

He spat again.

"Please continue," Mother said, "and I will be obliged if you direct the undertaker out to collect us. After what the bushwhackers did to me, it will be a relief to join my loved ones in death."

"Maybe you won't freeze before he gets here,"

the driver said. "Say, what's in the sack by the child's hand?"

"It's the poor boy's fiddle," she said. "It is the only thing the bushwhackers didn't take, and I intend to bury it with him."

"Guess they weren't music lovers."

"We can't leave her here," the partner said as he hopped down from the wagon. "She's hurt. You go on if you want, but I aim to help this woman."

He trudged through the snow. I could see now that he was a young man, in his early twenties, and he held the shotgun in the crook of his left arm. He grasped Mother gently by the elbow and coaxed her to her feet.

Mother swayed a bit, and then fell against him.

"Oh, I'm sorry," she said.

Then she withdrew the revolver from her pocket and placed it beneath the man's chin. Akers heard the sound of the cocking revolver, rose from the snow, and swiftly relieved the young man of his shotgun.

"Damn it all to hell," the driver said.

Akers cocked both barrels of the shotgun as he walked toward the wagon. The driver jumped from the seat, slipped in the snow, then got to his feet and produced an army revolver from his belt. He fired a quick shot, which missed, then hid behind the far side of the wagon.

"We need your rig," Akers shouted.

"So do we!" the driver shouted back.

"Drop your weapon or we'll kill your partner," Akers said.

"Go ahead and kill him," the mule skinner

shouted. "He's my nephew, but I never cared for him. I've been looking for a new partner anyway."

Mother kept the muzzle of the revolver pressed against the young man's chin. His eyes were wide in terror.

"Make him get down on the ground," Akers shouted to Mother. "You're too close to him. He could have a knife hidden. Besides, you don't want to get blood on you when you blow his head off."

"I don't have a knife!" the young man protested.

"Get down," Mother said.

"Don't kill me," he said, but remained on his feet. "Take the rig. We'll walk to Rolla." Then he brought his hands together in a pleading motion, and as he did he bumped Mother's elbow, and the Manhattan went off.

Blood splattered her face.

The young man fell to the ground, blood seeping from between his shattered jaw. Bits of bone glistened from where his nose had been, and one of his eyes had popped from its socket.

"Sonuvabitch," Akers said.

He dropped to the ground and fired one barrel of the shotgun into the snow beneath the wagon. The buckshot spread and cut the mule skinner's legs from beneath him.

The mules were startled, and they moved the wagon forward a few yards, leaving the man unprotected. He had dropped his revolver and was searching the snow for it.

Akers walked over to him and leveled the shotgun.

"Stu," Mother called. "Don't."

Akers kicked the revolver away from the mule skinner.

"Dammit all to hell," the man said. He tried to spit, but the tobacco juice just dribbled down the side of his face.

"We can't kill one and leave the other alive," Akers said.

He pulled the trigger and sent the remaining load of buckshot into the man's chest. Then he dropped the gun, grasped the man's feet, and pulled the body off the road by about twenty yards.

It left a crimson trail in the snow behind.

Then Akers returned and plucked the shotgun and the mule skinner's revolver from the snow. He placed the revolver in his belt and threw the shotgun onto the sacks of cornmeal in the bed of the freight wagon.

"The snow is a blessing," Akers said as he climbed up onto the seat and took the reins. "It will cover the bodies and hide the tracks of the wagon. We'll take the first crossroad and, with any luck, we'll be sixty miles away before anybody knows what happened here."

"Come on, Jacob," Mother said as she jerked me up from the snow. "Quit looking at him. It was an accident."

# Seventeen

I reckon I should feel bad about the two dead mule skinners we left on the road outside of Rolla, but I've never lost a moment's sleep over it. A tragedy was in the making, and it was simply a stroke of luck that resulted in them lying dead in the snow instead of us.

That's the way life is—a turn of the card.

No matter how you congratulate yourself on how well you've lived your life, it all comes down to luck. It begins with the accident of your birth and continues on until the last hand is dealt. Some of us are dealt considerably better hands at birth, of course, but that doesn't change the random nature of the game.

The thing that gives some folks an edge, however, is that they are determined to win, no matter how bad their situation might look. My mother was one of those people. She refused to admit defeat, never wasted time feeling sorry for herself, but instead immediately set about to identifying whatever advantages her new circumstances had conferred.

These qualities may seem manipulative and unladylike in polite society, but we had been in life-and-death situations since Mad Jack and his guerrillas burst into our cabin in Shelby County and demanded breakfast that morning in October. It set off a chain of clockwork events that propelled us farther and farther from what we had known, and Mother kept trying to beat the game every step of the way by redefining what it meant to win and lose.

Her thinking, I'm certain, worked something like this: Breakfast for guerrillas? A loss of only a little food and a few hours of sleep. Yankees burn down your cabin? Homes can be replaced. Husband about to be executed for riding with Porter? You set out with your twelve-year-old son to free him from the federal penitentiary. Husband dead after you've already traded sex for his release? You might as well save somebody since the bill has already been paid, and since it's your choice, he might as well be young and handsome. Sick, unable to walk, and freezing to death in the snow? Steal a wagon with some food. Mule skinner accidentally killed in the theft? Kill the other as well so that nobody can identity the guilty parties. Who, after all, were only doing what they had to do in order to survive.

That's what I pondered while I lay beneath a blanket in the bed of the freight wagon, on a mattress of cornmeal sacks, with my hands behind my head and looking up into the night sky. If you start at the beginning and take into account the entire chain of events, then morality becomes relative, and saving one life or ending another seems of equal value. Then I took the notion a step further—what if the life being forfeited is your own or that of someone dear to you instead of that of a stranger? That skewed things a bit. The only way the philosophy worked, then, was to stay alive.

But then, nobody lives forever, and when you die—early or late, in a comfortable bed or throat slit and left in a ditch—the chain goes on without you. Part and parcel of this, of course, is that there is no meaning to life, no grand design conferred by a creator, no parent in the unreachable sky who smiles approvingly at the good things you do and is heartbroken about the bad.

The German philosophers have come up with fancy labels for such thinking, of course, but none of them are very complimentary. But Mother must have found some comfort in her philosophy, and she would have said it was up to us to give life meaning. Even her fortune-telling could not shake her belief—even if a thing were preordained, the important thing was to make the best of the inescapable. Mother continually readjusted her considerable will to the problem at hand.

My problem, as I lay in the back of the wagon and looked up into a night sky filled with snowflakes, was that I did believe there was some larger meaning to life. Because Strachan had cut short my father's life, he must pay. So I remained trapped in my own hate, obsessed with the past and unable to meet with clear eyes the next link in the causal chain. My will was as hard as a diamond and focused with single intent on the killing of the bastard Strachan.

# Eighteen

At daylight, we found ourselves in a heavily wooded valley with a good stream, and we dared stop for a while. Akers made a tent of blankets under the boughs of an evergreen, and Mother crawled into it and was soon fast asleep.

Because I had had plenty of rest during the night in the bed of the wagon, I endeavored to help Akers with whatever tasks he now deemed necessary. The order of business was to catalog the contents of the wagon, cook up whatever we found for breakfast, and then to disguise the wagon so that it would not be recognized.

We had dozens of bags of cornmeal, of course, but also a few hams, a rasher of bacon, and several baskets of eggs. There were also the assorted pots needed to cook while on the road, salt, and a bit of sugar. But the thing that seemed to cheer Akers most was a can of Arbuckle's coffee.

There were more blankets and a sheet of canvas, a box of tools to take care of the wagon, including an ax and some saws and wrenches, and a bucket of axle grease. Grain for the mules.

Beneath the seat we found plenty: a pipe and tobacco, Lucifer matches, a ledger book, a couple of knives, and plenty of ammunition. There was powder, buckshot, percussion caps, and conical balls and paper cartridges for the army revolver. I was disappointed that there were no balls for the Manhattan, but Akers showed me that the buckshot was only slightly bigger than the .36-caliber balls required. Loading the revolver with loose powder and then ramming the buckshot home with the loading lever—which trimmed from the shot a bit of lead that resembled a fingernail clipping—made an acceptable load.

Akers made a circle of stones, built a fire, then dipped up a potful of snow. He placed the pot over the fire and, when the snow had turned to water and then begun to boil, he dumped in a handful of coffee. He rolled up some long corn dodgers and draped them over sticks near the fire, then proceeded to cook up the ham and eggs.

He took a plate of food and a cup of coffee to Mother's blanket tent, then returned to eat his breakfast with me. We sat on the back of the wagon and ate and, when we were finished, Akers loaded the found pipe with tobacco and lit it with one of the matches.

"My Lord," he said. "How I have missed tobacco and coffee."

"How I have missed bacon and eggs," I said.

"A beautiful morning," Akers said. "Look at how the dawn streaks the sky in pink and blue, and how the morning star fades in the west."

"Think it will snow again?" I asked.

"Surely," he said. "Look at those clouds—they remind me of my wife's lace curtains at home. It won't be long now until you see those for yourself."

"Your wife?"

"Yes," he said quickly. "She died. Jacob, hand me that ledger book and let's see if we can make any sense of it."

I handed him the book. He had already torn some of the pages out in order to start the fire. He flipped through the remaining sheets, about a third of which were filled with figures.

"Seems they were making a nice profit from the war."

Then he flipped to the front of the book.

"Their names—"

"I don't want to know," I said. "It doesn't matter."

"Do you want to know where they were from?"

"Yes," I said.

"Pulaski County," he said. "That's good, because it's up north a piece."

Then he tore the pages with writing out, crumpled them into a ball, and tossed it into the fire. He handed me the rest of the ledger.

"You could draw in it, or play games, if you so desire."

"Where are we now?" I asked.

"Shannon County, near the headwaters of the Current River," he said. "The trails will be rougher, but we're getting close to rebel country now."

"Does that mean we're safe?"

"Safer, anyhow," Akers said. "But we still had best change the appearance of the freight wagon a bit, just to err on the side of caution. We'll add some staves and other things to make it look different.

Not much we can do about the mules, though. They're not branded, but anybody with an eye for mules could recognize them."

"All mules look alike to me."

"Be careful around them," Akers said. "Let me feed 'em. They're a matched pair of jacks and they ain't been cut. They're mean, and might give us some trouble if they get a whiff of a mare in season. Not that they could do much about it, as they are all powder and no ball."

# Nineteen

Three days later, the snow had gone but the weather remained cold. We continued on in the freight wagon, which now had the canvas propped over it to make a tent, and Akers cussed the mules each time we had to ford a creek or negotiate a particularly tight turn on the increasingly narrow trail.

"Where are we?" Mother asked one day when we found ourselves in a deep, twisting valley where the trees leaned close and we could only see a narrow patch of sky above.

"Still in Missouri," Akers said. "But not by much."

"You mean we're lost?" she asked.

"We've been lost for the last couple of days," Akers admitted. "I kept thinking we would soon strike west, but the hills have been so wild that I'm afraid we won't be able to get the wagon over them. Best to keep moving until we find a good road."

"I thought you were from here," she said.

"I said I was from Kirbyville, in Taney County," he said. "I've never been here before. Few people have, from the looks of it. I don't remember the last time we passed a farm."

"These hills grow only rocks," Mother said.

It began to rain, and soon the rain turned to sleet. Mother and I took shelter beneath the tent in the bed of the wagon while Akers drove, his collar turned up and his hat pulled low.

Toward evening, we came to a broad but shallow stream at the base of a towering bluff. There was a broad cavern in the bluff, and Akers allowed that it would be a good place to stop for the night.

As Akers unhitched the team and cared for the mules, Mother gathered some wood and built a fire near the mouth of the cave so as to cook supper. The firelight illuminated a vast chamber with a clay floor, dotted with huge rocks that had fallen from the ceiling sometime in the ancient past.

I ventured far back into the cave, but Mother called to me.

"You'll stumble and crack your head on one these great rocks," she said. "Then where will we be? Stay close to the fire where I can keep an eye on you."

When Akers came in, his clothes were stiff with ice.

"You're going to freeze to death," she said.

Akers tried to speak, but could not. His mouth and beard were caked with frost.

Mother helped him out of his coat.

He walked stiffly to the fire, holding his palms to the warmth, but he could not control his shivering.

"The rest of them," Mother said.

"I'm fine," Akers managed through chattering teeth.

"You're not fine," she said. "Jacob, fetch some blankets."

I went to the wagon, climbed into the bed, and retrieved the requested items. When I returned, Mother was holding all of Akers's clothes over one arm. He was sitting naked on the rock, his boots on the clay beside him.

"Don't look so shocked," Mother said as she motioned for me to approach. "You saw your father unshucked, so it shouldn't surprise you that Mr. Akers has the same equipment."

I draped the blanket over his shoulders.

"Thank you," he said.

Then Mother made a disgusted face as she regarded the clothes in her hands. Then she looked down at her own stained dress, and then over at me.

"I reckon I'm a bit behind in my washing," she said. "Jacob, get the bucket from beneath the wagon and go down to the creek and scoop up some water. It's time that we all had a bath and some clean clothes."

"Take the revolver," Akers said.

"He will do no such thing," Mother said. "The temptation for the boy to play with the cursed thing would be too great, and we've already seen how accidents can happen."

"The boy has already proved himself a capable shot," Akers said. "He has taken plenty of small game."

"It is too dark to hunt rabbits."

"Your aversion has only seemed to develop after the incident on the road," Akers said.

"That is a subject of which I will not speak."

"Have you not noticed the other footprints here in the clay?" Akers asked.

"I paid them no mind," Mother said. "Who knows how long they have been here? They were probably made by some wild Indians long ago."

Akers nodded at the clay floor.

"These Indians," he said, "wear cavalry boots."

I went outside, got the bucket, and took care as I passed the mules. The freezing drizzle had stopped and the sky had cleared in the west. The sun had dipped behind the hills, but its rays shone still, turning the sky to gold.

Kneeling on the bank, I thrust my bucket into the water, breaking a thin coat of ice. When I brought it out, it contained a little water and a great portion of mud and gravel. I emptied the contents beside me and prepared to reach a little farther into the stream when I spied something unnatural in the mud I had just scooped from the river.

It was a bullfrog made from a blood-red stone.

I dipped the figure into the water and rinsed the mud away.

The frog was slightly smaller than my palm. It had large raised eyes, was crouching, and between its front feet was a ball of some kind. On the frog's back was a conical hole about the size of my thumb.

I put the frog in my pocket, scooped up a clean bucket of water, and hurried back to the cave. After I had placed the bucket next to the fire, I showed Akers the frog.

"I'll be damned," he said, examining the figure.

"I'm sure you will if you keep using that kind of language around my child," Mother said. Then she walked over and looked at the little statue Akers held.

"Where did you find that?" Mother demanded.

"I scooped it out of the mud," I said.

"Is it a toy?" she asked.

"It's a pipe," Akers said, putting his finger in the bowl on the frog's back. His hands were still shaking a bit from the cold. "And the stem went here, in the back. What a fine piece of work. Farmers sometimes find these in freshly plowed fields."

Mother picked it up.

"What does it have in its hands?"

"Who knows," Akers said. "The world, maybe."

"Did the Indians make this?"

Akers laughed.

"The boy has found a Biblical truth," he said. "It was made long ago, by one of the lost tribes of Israel. The contemporary redskin has forgotten how to work metal and stone and are mercifully ignorant of their Old Testament lineage. They still, however, maintain many Jew customs in their rituals, without knowing why."[1]

Mother blinked.

"Where do men get such notions?" she asked.

"It's authentic fact," Akers said. "Ask any learned man and he will tell you the same. The great mounds along the Mississippi River were made by the children of Abraham."

1. The belief that Native Americans were descendants of the lost tribes of Israel was a common nineteenth-century notion. The effigy pipe described resembles others found in late Mississippian period burial mounds from Illinois to Oklahoma, and would date from about 1300 A.D.

"You mean the children of Jacob," Mother said.

"I thought all Jews were descendants of Abraham."

"They are," Mother said, "but Abraham fathered both Isaac and Ishmael. The twelve Jewish tribes descend from Jacob, the favorite of the Isaac, while all Mohammedans spring from Ishmael, who was born of a dark-skinned slave girl."

"Of course," Akers said. "I have forgotten my Sunday School. So, is that why Jacob is named as such? To become the father of nations?"

"John Gamble named him," Mother said. "He was always taken with the story of Jacob wrestling the angel of God in the wilderness. But what were we debating?"

"The lost tribes."

"Oh, yes. How did the lost tribes cross the Atlantic Ocean when Christopher Columbus did not manage it until just three hundred and seventy years ago?"

"There were boats in Bible times."

"Men," she said. "How gullible."

"No more gullible than believing pasteboard cards can foretell the future," Akers said.

Mother gave him a stern look.

"Well, that's what Jacob told me," he said. "He said you had seen everything in the cards, from the Fallen Tower to the Hanged Man and the Devil himself. Do you deny it?"

"Jacob," Mother called. "Don't lie so."

"I didn't lie."

"He said that you had even seen me in your

cards, as the Knight of Wands, and that you were the Queen of Swords."

"I'm the Three of Swords," I said.

"What does all this foolishness mean?" he asked.

"Nothing," she said. "The cards are all burned up now, anyway, along with everything else in our cabin in Shelby County. They were just a silly gift from my mother. They meant nothing."

"What religion does your family hold?"

"We are Scotch Irish," she said. "Protestants."

"Not Catholics?"

"My mother was Catholic, but—"

"Has the boy been baptized?"

"No," she said. "But that hardly matters."

"It matters a great deal," Akers said passionately.

"Good Lord, you sound like the jailer back in Palmyra. That will be enough talk of religion," Mother said. "Not another word, I warn you."

"Can I keep it?" I asked.

"Keep what?" Mother asked impatiently.

"The bullfrog," I said. "Can I keep the bullfrog pipe?"

"It seems wicked to me," she said. "But I reckon it's all right, if Mr. Akers says it is from Bible times. Now get out of those clothes and prepare to get scrubbed."

I went to sleep that night clutching the frog.

Sometime after the fire had burned low and things were still, I roused to the sound of Mother washing her clothes in the bucket. She had a blanket over her shoulders, but was nude beneath, and I stared for a little while at her form.

Oh, don't look so shocked. Read your psychology.

When mother was done with the wash, she hung her clothes on the sticks she had placed near the fire, then went to Akers and slipped beneath the blanket with him.

# Twenty

Sometime before dawn, Akers shook me awake and told me to dress quickly.

"What's wrong?" I asked.

"Your mother is gone," he said.

I sat up, alarmed.

"Don't speak," Akers cautioned. He already had his boots and underwear on, and around his waist was his belt with a skinning knife and the army revolver. He held the shotgun across his knees, and was sliding the ramrod down each of the barrels to reassure himself that it was indeed loaded.

"There are men outside," he said softly. "I am going to confront them and I want you to stay here in the cave, far back in the shadows. Whatever happens, you are to remain hidden."

"No," I said.

"Don't argue with me, boy."

"How many are there?"

"Two," he said.

"Then you need me."

Akers paused.

"You keep out of sight," Akers said as he handed me the shotgun. "Do not shoot unless it is necessary, and even then, be sure of your target. If the worst happens, you are to run as far and as fast as you can."

I took up a position behind a pile of rocks at the mouth of the cave while Akers stole outside. The eastern sky had just begun to redden with the new day, and although the moon was still up, it was obscured by clouds. All I could see were shadows moving around the wagon and the mules.

It seemed like a long time before anything happened.

But I waited, with my heart in my throat, and my hands tight on the stock of the shotgun.

Then I saw the glint of Akers's knife, followed by the sickening sound of it being driven to the hilt into flesh and bone.

"You sonuvabitch," someone said.

A shot followed, and the flash from the muzzle lit the scene as if by lightning.

A man was on his knees, with Akers's knife in his stomach, and had discharged the pistol he held into the ground. Akers was standing before him, and had by now drawn and cocked the army, which was leveled at the man's head.

A rifle boomed from the other side of the wagon.

The ball slammed into the bluff overhead and showered pieces of rock down onto my hiding place.

"You missed," Akers said.

"Go to hell," came the reply.

"Have you another piece?" Akers shouted.

Then came the sound of running.

The moon emerged from behind the clouds, and I could see the man as he dashed down the trail toward the rocky ford. Akers stood with his feet apart, the army held in one hand, and he fired, without apparent effect.

The man was some thirty yards away as Akers cocked the revolver again, took aim, and pulled the trigger. The target staggered, but remained upright.

Akers fired a third round.

This time the man clutched his chest, wheeled, and fell backward into the water.

"Jacob, are you all right?"

"Yes, sir," I said.

"Keep that scattergun trained on that one on the ground," he said. "But don't kill him yet."

I moved out from behind the rocks and stood over the man with the knife in his gut while Akers walked out to where the other had fallen in the river.

He stepped into the shallow water, the moonlight gilding the ripples, and put the heel of his boot on the man's chest. The action elicited a pitiful moan.

Akers put a round into his head.

Then he walked back, put the army in his belt, and took the shotgun from me.

"You did a fine job," he said.

The man on the ground gritted his teeth and clutched the knife with both hands, attempting to pull it free. He screamed in pain and gave up the effort.

Akers squatted next to him.

"It's deep," Akers said, cradling the shotgun. "I could feel it glance off bone when I drove it in.

You're so damned thin it may have gone all the way to your spine."

The intruder grimaced.

Akers picked up the pistol the man had fired into the ground. It was a massive old single-shot with an octagonal barrel that was dark with rust.

"A poor tool for this kind of work."

Akers slung the pistol into the brush.

It was a little lighter now. The birds were beginning to stir, and the wind blew from the north, rustling the frosted branches of the trees. I could see that the man on the ground was dressed in tattered clothes, and wore an old pair of shoes that were held together by rags.

"Where's the woman?" Akers asked.

The man was silent.

Akers grasped the hilt of the knife and shook it.

The man convulsed. His eyes rolled back in his head and blood trickled from the corner of his mouth.

"I asked you a question," Akers said.

"Across the river," he said.

"Where across the river?"

"A big oak just on the far side. The others wait there."

"How many of you remain?"

"Three," he said.

"Why take her?"

"She surprised us," he said. "She apparently was heeding nature's business. Fought like hell and she was spirited away lest she wake you in the cave."

"Why didn't you kill us while we slept?" Akers asked.

"Afraid," he said. "Soldiers use the cave. We didn't know your number or how well you were armed."

He closed his eyes.

"Please," he said. "No more."

Akers placed his boot on the man's chest, reached down with both hands, and wrenched the knife free. It made a ghastly sucking sound as it came out.

Then we heard splashing, and we turned to see Mother wading the ford. She was still in her night-clothes. Her hands were bound, and her mouth was gagged by a strip of filthy cloth.

We rushed down to meet her, and Akers freed her hands with the bloody knife. Before she even took the cloth from her mouth, she wrapped both arms around me.

"Are they gone?" Akers asked.

She nodded.

"Are you well?"

She tugged the gag away.

"I am bruised, but otherwise unhurt."

Akers then hugged the both of us.

"I thought I had lost you," he said.

"And if you had?" she queried.

"Don't know how I could have gone on."

"Then let me tell you what I expect," she said, "You will go on, no matter what. You are to get the boy to safety and provide him a home, with all that implies."

"Of course," Akers said.

A few minutes ago, Akers had been a righteous killer and taught me volumes about the power of decisive action. Now, reunited with Eliza Gamble, he again assumed his deferential role in the partnership.

Mother hesitated, believing perhaps that she had

gone too far with the lecture. So she brightened, cocked her head a bit, and smiled.

"I owe you my life," she said. "Thank you."

"No, Eliza," he said. "It is I who owe my life to you. The truth is that I was the only one of the ten at Palmyra who truly deserved to die—I was not so much an irregular soldier as a thief and a murderer. You have only seen my former self twice since then, once on the road and now again here."

"I prefer your former self," she said.

Akers demanded an explanation.

"The kidnappers watched by moonlight as you shot their man at the river," she said. "I was afraid they would kill me for spite, but their will deserted them and they ran like rabbits."

# Twenty-one

After we crossed the river, we turned west, the hills smoothed, and the going became a bit easier. In the valleys, we began to encounter small signs of civilization—a farm here, a lonely cabin there—and while the occupants watched us pass with suspicion, we detected little hostility.

The weather warmed and we all rode up front, watching the scenery as we rolled slowly through it. The weather had turned unexpectedly warmer, as it sometimes does in the Ozarks in late October and early November. The land was shrouded in muted shades of brown and orange, and with not a trace of green save for the cedars that clustered in draws and clung to gentle slopes.

About mid-morning of the third day, Mother asked Akers to stop for a spell. He pulled the wagon to a stop, set the brake, and asked what was the matter.

"Nothing," she said. "I just feel a bit ill. Probably something I ate disagreed with me, or the constant jostling of the wagon."

Then she put her hand to her mouth, scooted to the edge of the seat, and heaved over the side of the wagon.

Akers looped the reins around the brake handle.

"Come on, Jacob," he said. "I'll show you something that might help ease the pain in your mother's stomach."

He led me onto the nearest hillside and searched the ground among the timber.

"What are you looking for?" I asked.

"This," he said, seizing the trunk of a scrubby tree.

He fell to the ground at the base of the tree and began digging with his knife into the dirt. Soon, the tree's yellow roots were exposed, and he hacked until he had freed a clump.

"Sassafras," he said, shaking the dirt from the roots.

He placed the roots on a rock and chopped them into cork-sized chunks. When he was done, he scooped them up and poured them into my hand.

Exposed to the air, the roots had turned a deep orange. They gave off a pleasant aroma, which reminded me a little of coffee and a little of licorice.

"It's medicine," he said. "The old women gather it in the spring and make a tonic from it, but it's good at any time of the year."

When we returned to the wagon, he built a small fire, poured the roots and some water into a pot, and hung the pot over the fire on a stick.

"I don't think that will help," Mother protested from the wagon as she watched Akers work. Her arms were folded across her stomach and her face was quite pale.

"It can't hurt," Akers said.

The water boiled, and soon Akers had sassafras tea. He poured the tea into a couple of tin cups, and added a pinch of sugar into each.

"Here," he said, as he handed me the cup. "It's good for you. Be careful, for it is hot."

I held the cup in both hands, with my jacket cuffs protecting my palms, and blew on the surface. Then I took a sip and was surprised at how pleasant and mild it tasted.

Mother held hers up carefully by the handle, brought it to her nose, and then made a face.

"I can't drink this," she said. "It makes me gag."

Then she slung the contents of the cup over the side.

"Suit yourself," Akers said. "I was just trying to help."

"I'll be fine, I'm sure," she said, holding her head in her hands. "I felt this way once before, and it finally passed."

"How long did that take?"

"Let's waste no more time," Mother said, ignoring his question. "Gather up those things and let's be on our way."

The next day, Mother was again sick in the morning.

She asked Akers to stop so that she could have a little relief from the motion of the wagon. As he reined the team to a stop, he asked her if she wanted to climb down and walk about a bit.

"No," she said. "Just give me a few minutes."

"You won't have to suffer much longer," Akers said. "I know this country now. We're nearing the White River Valley, and things will get steeper and more wooded again. Soon, we'll cross the old salt road between Springfield and northern Arkansas."

As we waited, a group of riders approached from the west.

Akers slipped the army from his belt and placed it behind him, beneath a blanket in the bed of the wagon, and asked me to do the same with the shotgun.

"Where is the Manhattan?" he asked Mother.

"In my pocket, of course," she said.

"Refrain from reaching for it," he said.

"We are to meet these men unprotected?" she asked.

"We will keep the weapons handy, but will show no hint that we are armed," he said. "It is a Yankee patrol and I do not wish to provoke them to action."

Akers took the reins and pulled the wagon over to the side of the road, giving the soldiers room to pass without forcing them to take the brush. Then he set the brake with his foot and waited.

There were a dozen or so troopers, wearing dark blue blouses and sky-blue trousers with yellow stripes, and they were all young. Each had a revolver in a flap holster and, either hanging from the saddle or clutched in their gloved hands, a carbine.

"Good morning," said the lieutenant as he brought his horse close to the wagon.

"Morning," Akers said, and tugged at the brim of his hat.

"Traders?" the officer asked, eyeing the wagon.

"Were," Akers said. "The secesh burned us out of our home in Shannon County and we are on our way to stay with kin at Springfield. What news do you have? Does the Union still hold the city?"

"For now," the lieutenant said.

"At least we can be thankful of that," Akers said.

"There are rumors that Marmaduke is courting trouble along the Arkansas border and will soon strike north, if he hasn't already," the lieutenant said. "That is why we are on patrol. Have you seen anything that might increase our intelligence?"

"We encountered some bushwhackers near the Current River," Akers said. "But they were poorly outfitted and hardly seemed a part of any regular command. Deserters, most likely."

"The hills are full of them," the lieutenant said.

"Other than that, we've had the road to ourselves," Akers said.

One of the mules shook its head and brayed.

"Is this your wife and child?"

"Yes," Akers said.

"How do you do," Mother said. "The boy's name is Jacob."

"What's your last name, Jacob?"

"Sir?" I asked.

"Your last name," he said.

"You'll have to forgive the boy," Mother said. "He is quite slow. Jacob, can you tell the officer how old you are?"

"Twelve," I said.

"No," Mother said. "You're eleven, remember?"

Mother shook her head, as if ashamed at my stupidity.

"What's your name, madam?" the lieutenant asked.

"Elizabeth Dunbar," she said. "My husband is John. We are so happy to meet you, Major, because frankly we have been scared to death since leaving

Shannon County. Now John, don't argue. You know how anxious you get."

"I'm a lieutenant, madam."

The mules shuffled, and the wagon slid a yard or so as they pulled against the brake.

"Pardon me," Akers said, "but the mules have not been gelded. One of your mares is in season, I believe."

The lieutenant turned in the saddle.

"Sullivan," he called. "Ride on up the road a hundred yards and wait for us."

"Yes, sir," the trooper said, and urged the mare forward. He stopped at the crest of a low hill, silhouetted against the sky.

"Dunbar," the lieutenant said. "The telegraph at Springfield chattered with news a fortnight ago that a freight wagon and its team had been stolen outside of Rolla, and that the two mule skinners were murdered and their bodies left in the snow. I seem to recall that the wire said the mules in the team had not been gelded."

"I wouldn't know about that," Akers said.

"That rig certainly looks like a freight wagon."

"As I said, we were traders."

"I don't recall traders wearing such clothes as yours," the lieutenant said. "Your coat has a rather military look to it, and I have seen many guerrillas wear shirts with embroidered roses similar to yours."

"It is a hunting shirt, like others," Akers said. "It is a tradition in the county. As to the coat, I traded for it and have no idea of its origin."

The lieutenant sat his horse and stared at Akers.

Instead of matching his gaze, Akers looked away. Then the lieutenant produced his revolver.

"What's in the bed of the wagon?"

"You'll find a ham and sacks of meal," Akers said. "Some other goods we managed to salvage from the fire. If you're hungry, you're welcome to take what you want."

"We have our rations," the lieutenant said.

"He said there was ham," a corporal spoke up.

"I heard what he said. You take one of the men and search the bed of the wagon." Then the lieutenant turned back to Akers. "Is there anything you'd like to tell me now?"

Akers pursed his lips.

"Can't think of a damned thing," he said.

Then he brightened.

"Oh, I almost forgot," he said. "I do have a jug of whiskey that I'd be obliged if you'd take. Just to keep the chill off. It can get mighty cold in these woods at night."

"Against regulations for the men."

"But not for you," Akers said, and reached behind the seat as the troopers climbed into the bed.

But before Akers could produce the revolver, a rifle shot rang out behind us. We turned to see the soldier who had ridden ahead falling from the saddle.

"Looks like Sullivan found a rebel patrol," Akers said. "Or rather, they found him."

The lieutenant cursed.

"Mount up," he shouted at the men in the wagon.

As they scrambled for their horses, a half-dozen mounted soldiers topped the hill behind us. We could not discern what color they wore, but from their actions there was little doubt.

"Get out of here," the lieutenant said. "This is no place for a woman and child."

Akers touched his hat, released the brake, and whipped the team. The wagon lurched forward.

"Form up," the lieutenant shouted.

As the Yankee cavalry advanced, the rebels turned their horses and fled. The lieutenant gave chase. We were a quarter of a mile away when the rattle of many guns echoed behind us.

"The fools have ridden into a trap," Akers said.

"I hope they kill them all," Mother said.

# Twenty-two

As Akers had predicted, the land once again turned wild. The next day, the hills became steep and the road became narrower and rockier. Late in the afternoon, it began to rain, and we found ourselves attempting to mount a particularly sharp and muddy incline that led to a high saddle.

We had nearly reached the top of the grade when a rear wheel of the wagon became mired in a depression. The mules balked, and although Akers stung them with the whip and made them strain against the harness, they could not pull the wheel from where it had sunk.

"Dammit," Akers said.

He took off his hat, wiped his forehead with his sleeve, then turned his face to the rain, catching a little water in his mouth. Then he spat, and handed Mother the reins.

"The wheel is fast against a rock," he said. "While Jacob and I push, I want you to drive the team. Don't spare the whip or we'll never get the wagon out of this hole."

I jumped to the ground behind Akers, my shoes splashing in the mud. The iron rim of the left rear wheel was deep in the mud. Akers dropped to his knees and searched the hole with his hand.

"It's not a rock," he said. "It's a ledge."

Akers got to his feet, planted his boots, and gripped the spokes of the wheel.

"Jacob, shove against the back of the wagon when I tell you."

Akers took a breath and shouted, "Now."

We strained against the wagon while Mother wildly drove the team. The mules struggled, their hooves slipping and clattering on the slick road, and the wagon rose a bit, but slid sideways before it could overcome the ledge.

"Stop," Akers shouted.

The wagon rolled back, knocking me to the ground.

Akers shook his head as he grabbed me by the collar of my coat and pulled me to my feet.

"Careful," he said.

"You need some leverage," Mother called back.

"We almost had it," Akers called. "Let's try again, and really crack the whip on those stubborn bastards. Once more, Jacob, and really put your back into it this time."

I braced myself and placed my palms against the tailgate.

Akers crouched lower, grasped a spoke in each hand, and shouted for Mother to drive. The mules brayed, I pushed with everything I could muster, and Akers cussed through lips that were tight with the strain. The wheel rose again on the ledge, then stopped.

"Drive!" Akers shouted.

I heard the snap of the whip, the cries of the mules, and the grunts that Akers emitted as he attempted to push the wagon beyond the last critical inch.

Then there was a terrible crack as the wheel broke and the corner of the wagon fell, crushing Akers beneath it. I jumped away as the wagon slid backward and pivoted sideways, carrying the team with it, and then Mother was thrown from the seat as the wagon slowly turned over.

The wagon fell to pieces when it hit the ground, scattering the contents of the bed into the mud, and sending one of the wheels bouncing back down the road. The linchpin had given way and, now free, the mules had raced over the hill, dragging the wagon tongue behind them.

Akers lay faceup in the mud, his chest crushed and a broken spoke piercing his right side. Blood ran from his nose and mouth, and with his every breath there was a terrible gurgling sound.

Mother, who had landed unhurt in the water and muck of the road, got to her feet and stumbled over to Akers. She stood over him and trembled, her hands clasped to her mouth.

The rain was heavier now, and it washed the blood in rivulets back down the road to the east.

Akers looked up at her and smiled.

"Stupid way to die," he said through the blood.

"No," Mother said, dropping beside him and taking his hand in hers. "You can't die, you can't, not after all we've been through, not from an accident, not on this road, not after our journey was nearly done, you cannot die."

Akers tried again to speak, but all that came from his mouth was a blood bubble that grew and then burst. Then his eyes went dim and he died staring into my mother's face.

# Twenty-three

*From Donovan's notes*

Gamble pushed his plate away. There was nothing left but bone and gristle. Then he grasped the mug of black coffee, and weighed it in his hand. For a moment, I was afraid he would throw it. Then he took a sip and carefully placed the mug back on the table.

"So you and your mother were alone again," I said.

"We weren't alone," he said. "We had each other."

"What did you do?"

"Well, Mother wouldn't move for some time," he said. "She couldn't leave him. I had never before seen her completely shaken, unable to act, or even to speak. So I searched through the remains of the wagon and gathered up some things I thought we would need. I found the shotgun, but the barrels were twisted and ruined, so I tossed it aside. I could not find the army revolver."

"What about the fiddle?" I asked suspiciously.

"It survived the wreck," he said. "I found it alongside the road, still in the burlap sack which we had placed it in to protect it from the rain and snow."

"That seems a miracle," I said.

"No," he said. "It would have been a miracle had the fiddle been destroyed and Akers had lived. But it seemed that God had little to do with the affair."

The House of Lords was absolutely throbbing with activity, and I had scooted my chair close to Gamble in order to hear. The clink of plates and glasses, the clatter of the telephone behind the bar, and the sound of a hundred conversations all going at once had combined in a muted roar. Over in the corner, a piano player was doing his best to make Cole Porter's "Night and Day" heard above the din.

"Nice tune," Gamble said, and placed his hand on my knee.

"They used to play ragtime," I said.

Then the bar suddenly quieted. The music died. The patrons parted to allow a couple of men in smart suits to make their way to the center of the room.

The men stood uncomfortably for a moment. The tall one shoved his hands in his pockets and waited with shoulders stooped, a kind of an *aw-shucks*, while the younger man with the bright face smiled and I felt my heart skip a beat.

Then the owner of the place, Joe Dorizzi, came out from behind the bar. He motioned for the bartender to hand him a bung starter.

"Ladies and gentlemen," Dorizzi said, then rapped the counter with the little wooden hammer. "Ladies and gentlemen! You all know that the new RKO release *Hellfire Canyon* premiered here in

Joplin last night. May I introduce the stars of that talking picture, John Huston and Tyrone Power."

The bar erupted in applause. The piano player felt his way around a few bars of "Sweet Betsy from Pike," which had been the film's wildly inappropriate theme.

"They even got that wrong," Gamble muttered.

Huston held out his broad hands to the crowd.

"Thank you," he said. "Please, don't let us interrupt your fun. I am pleased at the warm reception Missouri has given us, and for me it is a welcome homecoming. I grew up in Los Angeles, but was born in Nevada. My grandfather won the entire damn town in a poker game once, but I'm told the city fathers are reluctant now to part with my birthright."

He paused for effect.

"I assure you that if Grandfather had won Joplin in that poker game," he said, "I would not be going back to southern California so soon."

The crowd roared its approval.

"Here is the real star," Huston said, pushing the shy young man at his side a few steps forward. "My career is over, considering the reaction of the studio to my film, but young Tyrone has just begun. I'm sure you'll see much more of his handsome face in the years ahead."[1]

I stood.

"Mr. Huston," I said, a bit nervously.

---

1. Tyrone Power came back to Missouri and, with Henry Fonda, shot *Jesse James* on location at Pineville in 1938. The small Ozark town, located about forty miles south of Joplin, still celebrates the film with Jesse James Days each August. No similar event celebrating *Hellfire Canyon* was ever suggested for Joplin.

"Ah, the young reporter," Huston said. "Fine article in today's paper. Did I tell you that I worked at the *New York Graphic* briefly? I was fired, and rightly so—I was the lousiest reporter that ever lived."

"I'm sure you exaggerate," I said.

"That was my problem," he said.

More laughter.

"There's someone I think you should meet," I said.

"But of course, my dear," Huston said. He was not yet thirty, and Hollywood had deemed his long face a handicap. While he may have been ugly as sin, he was charming as hell.

"May I introduce the outlaw Jacob Gamble?"

Both of them stared.

"You mean the *real* Jacob Gamble?" Power asked.

"Yes," I said. "The man you portray in the film. He says he was rather younger at the time, however."

Huston broke into a very broad grin.

"What're you drinking?" he asked, dragging Tyrone to the table with him. "Whatever it is, we'll have two of 'em."

Gamble stood, looked Huston in the eye, and I was afraid for a moment that the pair wouldn't shake hands. Then Gamble offered his left hand, and Huston clutched it warmly in both of his paws.

"What an unexpected surprise," he said.

Then Tyrone shook Gamble's hand, and as they looked around for a place to sit, the patrons around him offered a dozen chairs at once.

"Thank you," Huston said. "But we require only two."

Huston slid one of the chairs across the floor to Tyrone, and then he took the other, planted it near

Gamble and me, and sat with his arms across the back, looking from face to face.

"Tyrone," he said. "Any more cigars?"

"You cleaned me out an hour ago, you maniac," Tyrone said amiably.

"Allow me," Gamble said, and produced two cigars from his vest pocket. "They're cheap," he said, "so don't expect much."

Huston plucked one from Gamble's hand, bit the end off and spat it out, and struck a match on the table. As he sucked great clouds of smoke into his lungs, he smiled and rapped his knuckles on the seat back.

"This is just what I wanted," he said. "First decent smoke I've had since arriving here. My compliments, Mr. Gamble."

"Jacob," he said.

"All right," Huston said. "Call me John."

The Irish waiter came and cleared the table, then brought double whiskeys for everyone.

"The drinks," he said, "are on the house."

Huston clapped his hands in delight.

"Now, that's what I like to hear."

Huston inclined his head conspiratorially toward Gamble, took another puff on the cigar, and said through the smoke, "We were told you were dead."

"Is that why you didn't ask my opinion?"

"Of course, old boy," Huston said.

"I was told I was dead more than once," Gamble said. "But I'm still kickin'. This girl reporter, this Frankie Donovan, tracked me down from my records at the state pen at Jefferson City."

When he pronounced my name, he mimicked an Irish accent—*Doonavan*.

"So you are an outlaw," Huston said. "Served time. For what?"

"For those things you normally serve time in prison for."

"Bank robbery?"

"Yes"

"Murder?"

"Never," Gamble said. "At least, I never killed anybody who didn't deserve it."

"That's his story, anyway," I said, and the men laughed.

"Mind a few questions, Mr. Gamble?" Huston asked.

"As long as I'm allowed to return the favor."

"What is your impression of my film?"

"The title is dreadful—"

"Blame the studio for that."

"Most of the details are wrong," Gamble said. "I was just thirteen in 1862, and my mother isn't even in the story. But Tyrone Power is much prettier than I am, so I'll have to say that I was well cast after all."

Huston laughed.

I was feverishly taking shorthand.

"But what of Alf Bolin?" Huston asked. "Did we get it right there? How far were we from the mark?"

"You are ten years older than Bolin," Gamble said, "But your looks and mannerisms are uncanny similar. There's something about the way your hold yourself erect, the way you use your hands, and the speeches you give—"

"I knew it would have been a mistake to portray Bolin as an illiterate woodsman," Huston said to

Tyrone. "I'm glad we fought to leave the monologues in."

"Nothing beats instinct," Tyrone agreed meekly.

"But what can you tell me of the real Bolin?" Huston asked, then drained the double in one long draw, and a bit of whiskey dribbled down his chin. "What kind of man was he?"

"Bolin had no conscience," Gamble said. "He was a smart, well-spoken, and likeable monster who killed people for sport. Men, women, children—it didn't matter, at least not to him. He stole fortunes in gold and silver and had no place to spend it. He led a band of thirteen cutthroats that was nearly as wicked as him, but not nearly as smart."

"I thought his band numbered only twelve," Tyrone said.

"That's where your story is wrong," Gamble said. "I know, because I was the thirteenth member of the gang."

"Ah," Huston said. "If only we'd had this material while I was writing the damned script."

Then an argument broke out at the bar.

A drunken miner was screaming at the top of his lungs at a banker who had been unlucky enough to walk by on his way back to his table after using the gentlemen's room.

"Think you're something, don't you?" the miner shouted.

The drunk man wasn't dressed in work clothes, and he did not carry a pail or helmet, but I had seen him in the bar before, and I knew he was a miner because he continually carped about his shift at the St. Joseph Lead and Zinc Company. His name was Carl and he was a likeable sort until well drunk, when he would recount in great detail his troubles with the bank for anyone who cared to listen, and for many who didn't.

"Listen, you pasty-faced Hooverite sonuvabitch," the miner said, stabbing his finger into the banker's rotund chest. "I will burn that house on Empire Street to the ground before I let the bank take it back."

The banker waved his hand dismissively.

"I swear, I will light a match and—"

"Perhaps we should do something," Huston suggested.

"Wait and watch," I said. "It's a nightly ritual, and is about to come to an end."

The bartender came up behind the agitated miner and tapped him smartly on the head with the bung starter. The miner blinked once, then slumped to the floor.

As the bartender was dragging the man by his feet toward the back door, I suggested to Huston and the others that we should drink fast.

"Always good advice," Huston said. He was by now famously drunk. "But why the haste?"

"Carl will come around in a minute or two," I said. "And when he does, he'll put his fist through the electric meter in the alley, taking out the lights."

Huston laughed.

"To Carl!" he said, holding his drink high.

"To Carl!" we chorused, raising our drinks.

We slammed our glasses on the tabletop.

Then there was a loud bang, the tinkle of glass, and the lights in the House of Lords flickered and then went out.

# Twenty-four

I left my mother on the road beside Akers's body.

A calculated risk, to be sure, but nothing I had said would make her speak or even look at me. What was I to do? The wagon was wrecked, the team had fled, and the weather was still miserable. We were not far from Taney County, Akers had said, so I threw the sack with the fiddle over my shoulder and began walking the rest of the way up the hill.

If there was one thing I had learned during our travail, it was that decision was necessary in the face of despair. I hoped that Mother would follow my example and continue on, but I had no guarantee.

At the crest of the hill I looked back, and my mother had not turned to watch my departure. She was still wearing the coat she had taken from the dead guerrilla, the rain had plastered her red hair tightly against her head and neck, and her hands lay impotently in her lap.

My stomach was in knots, but I forced myself to continue over the hill. A broad dark valley lay before me, and I had to force each step forward. It was as if my whole body was in rebellion, longing to return, but I drove the fear from my mind and pressed on.

A mile on, I heard my mother call to me.

I paused, waiting for her to catch up.

"You could have waited," she said.

"No, I couldn't," I said.

"We should have buried him," she said. "He at least deserved that much."

"And more," I said. "But how were we going to bury him? Were we to make a shallow grave and dump his body into it, unmarked? Perhaps we could have waited for the next group of soldiers to arrive, and then we would be discussing the matter in the stockade at Springfield."

"It still doesn't make it right."

"Somebody will find the wreck and bury him," I said. "They will do a better job than we could have, I reckon. But Akers feels nothing now—neither pain, nor embarrassment, nor any requirement for ritual—although I cannot say the same for us."

Mother hugged her arms to her chest as she walked.

"How were you sure I would follow?" she asked.

"I wasn't."

# Twenty-five

We followed the wild path as it snaked through the hills, slept in caves and drank water from the streams, and along the way we encountered others on the road. They were refugees, like ourselves, with gaunt faces and hollow eyes, nearly all of them on foot. When we neared, they shuffled to the far side of the road, averted their eyes, and passed without a word of greeting.

Within three days, we found ourselves in Kirbyville. It wasn't a town, at least not the kind that we were used to back home, but a collection of rough buildings on either side of the muddy road. There were a few businesses, chiefly a blacksmith and a livery, and a post office located in a mercantile.

There were also a couple of taverns, and these were the only businesses in town that seemed to be going concerns. In the little time since we had entered the town, a dozen Yankee soldiers had either emerged from or disappeared into the dark buildings. Outside, in the street, there were a few women hanging about who looked much like the refugees we had passed on the road, except these women looked much more hopeless.

"You must stay away from such places," Mother told me.

Mother smoothed her skirt, batted the dirt from her coat, and opened the door to peer inside the one-room mercantile. The shelves were all but empty. The ugly black stove along the back wall crackled, but it was poorly tended, and smoke hung in the air like fog.

Mother coughed and fanned the door to get some fresh air into the room.

"Shut the door," an old man said.

He sat in a rocking chair, smoking a corncob pipe and pondering a checkerboard that lay on the top of a barrel beside him.

Mother closed the door behind us, and cautiously crossed the plank floor to the old man. I followed, gawking at the array of items that hung from the wall behind the counter: the skulls of squirrels, rabbits, and foxes; rattlesnake hides that had been tacked flat and were at least as long as a man is tall; and other bits of hair and bone that I could not identify.

"Strangers," the old man said.

"Not to our friends," Mother said.

"You'll find no friends here," the old man said. "I've had my fill of folks coming and begging for necessities when they have no coin in their pocket. Even if they did, there's little I could sell them now. Few supplies have come since the war began."

"We're not looking for charity," Mother said. "We seek the Akers cabin. The sign in your window proclaims that you are the postmaster, so I assumed you would be able to tell us where to find it."

"What's your business?" the old man asked.

"Family business," Mother said.

The old man looked up from the checkerboard. "Kin?" he asked.

"I will not discuss family business with a stranger," she said. "As you said, we have no friends here. If you cannot or will not tell us, please say so and we will find someone else in town to give us directions."

"Does the boy know how to play checkers?" he asked.

"Of course," I said.

"Play me a game of checkers and if you win, I'll give your mother the directions," he said.

"What if he loses?" mother asked.

"Then you will be no poorer than you are now."

Mother sighed.

"All right," she said, and removed her coat. "But you must let me tend to the stove. It is infernally hot, and I am about to gag from the smoke. Have you not noticed?"

"I'm cold all the time," the old man said. "I just let 'er burn full blast. But suit yourself."

While Mother went to the stove, I slipped out of my own coat, placed the sack with the fiddle on the floor, and sat on a stool on the other side of the board.

The old man beamed.

He let me move first. I had played checkers with my father, as all boys do, but had never developed an enthusiasm for the game. It seemed rather silly to me, and any good player should at least be able to force a draw. The old man played slowly, thinking about each move for a long time, but inhaling all of that smoke must have dulled his mind, for he made two stupid moves that he was never able to recover from.

The old man grumbled.

"I'm sure you let the boy win," Mother said. "How kind of you. Now, the directions."

The old man tapped out his pipe against the palm of his hand, letting the cold ashes fall to the floor.

"Take the coach road north around Snapp Balds," he said. "Before you reach the ferry crossing on the White River, you'll find a path that takes off down—"

He stopped.

"Whose spread were you looking for?"

"Akers," Mother said impatiently.

"Why didn't you say so?" he asked. "Hell, I thought you wanted the Bakers. You'll find the Akers place three miles south on the coach road. Turn to the west when you see a pile of rocks that looks like an elephant, and the cabin is not a quarter of a mile beyond. But don't go any farther south than the elephant rock or you'll wind up on Pine Mountain, and nobody wants to be *there*."

"Why not?" mother asked.

"Alf Bolin, that's what's wrong," the old man said. "Damn, you are a pretty little fool. You go down there, and Bolin will slit your throats."

Mother motioned for me, and I grabbed my things.

"You might want to let a little air in here," she said over her shoulder as we made our way to the door. "The smoke has cured your brains."

"Hey," he shouted.

He took a couple of apples from a sack beneath his chair.

"Good game, son. Play me again when you come back this way."

He tossed the apples to us.


By mid-afternoon, we found the cabin.

It was not exactly a shack, but it was modest even by Ozark standards and in need of repair. The yard was untended, and if there hadn't been smoke drifting from the chimney, we might have assumed it was unoccupied. Although there was a barn out back, we saw no livestock. But on the porch was a hound, and it bayed to announce our approach.

"Don't worry, Jacob," she told me. "Everything will be all right once we explain things to Stu's parents. I just wish we had brought better news."

Mother ignored the dog as we walked up the wooden steps onto the porch. She knocked, then waited as the hound snarled at us from the far end of the porch.

There were footsteps inside the cabin, and I saw a woman peek at us from behind a curtain. Then we heard the bolt being drawn and the door opened.

The woman had sharp features and a small mouth, and on her hip was a dirty child of about two years. The child had thin dark hair, like its mother, and I could not tell if it was a boy or a girl.

"Yes?" the woman asked.

"Pardon us," Mother said, "but is this the Akers place?"

"What do you want?" the woman asked suspiciously.

The child began to cry, and the woman jiggled it.

Mother looked past the woman to the interior of the cabin. There seemed to be no one else around.

"Are you alone?" she asked.

"You see anybody else?"

The child began to cry, and the woman tugged at her blouse and offered it her breast. I could not help but stare as the child suckled greedily.

"You want the other one?" she asked.

I quickly looked away.

"Could we speak to Mr. Akers, or the missus?" she asked.

"I'm the missus," she said curtly. "If you're looking for Stu, he's off playing soldier. I haven't seen him in about a year. What do you know of Stu, anyway?"

Mother smiled tightly.

"I'm sorry," she said. "I don't know a Stu Akers. We were looking for the home of our cousin, Samuel Akers, and were directed here by the postmaster at Kirbyville. I can see now that he was mistaken."

"Don't know any Samuel Akers in these hills," the woman said. "Ain't got no kin by that name, neither. Sure you got the right part of the country?"

"I'm sure we don't," Mother said, backing away from the door and taking me with her. The hound beneath the porch continued to snarl. "Please, forget we were here."

We walked back down the path to the coach road. Mother found a stump at the base of the elephantine border, sat down, and placed her head in her hands.

Then she laughed.

"We've come so far," she said. "What could Stu have been thinking of? Was he going to move us all into the shack and have us adopt the Mormon doctrine?"

"It will be dark in a few hours," I said.

"What a hideous woman," she said. "What shrewish features! And that filthy child. I know they may be short of food, but there seems to be no lack of water in these hills or wood to heat it with. We carry dirt from the road, I know, but when one is at home, there is no excuse for not bathing."

"We'd best head back to Kirbyville," I said. "There's more rain coming. We could find a dry place to sleep, perhaps in the livery."

"And the customs here!" she said. "She had no more modesty than a sow. Not that it will help that little pig of a child, because it will surely starve at that table."

"They don't know any better," I said. "Our best bet now is to head north to Springfield. I know it is full of Yankees, but they're well provisioned. They cannot possibly identify us as those that took the wagon, not without Mr. Akers to bring suspicion upon us."

"No," Mother said. "I want no more Yankees. We will continue south, to Arkansas, where the rebels yet rule. What do you know of Springdale, Jacob?"

"Nothing," I said, "except that it is some distance."

"We have come this far," she said. "What's another few miles?"

"I believe it is farther than that," I said. "And

remember what the postmaster said about Pine Mountain?"

"Ah, the postmaster was an addled old fool," she said.

"It is time to give up the road," I said. "Your sickness increases in the morning, we have no food, and winter is hard upon us."

She stood, smoothed her coat, and set off to the south.

I stood in the middle of the rutted road and cursed passionately. I used all of the words that I had heard Akers use with the mules, and invented a few of my own. I kicked rocks, stamped my feet, and invited God to strike me dead instead of subjecting me to further misery.

"Do it!" I shouted at the sky. "There are already storm clouds on the horizon. It would take little effort to summon a bolt of lightning to punish my blaspheme."

I stretched my arms wide, turned my face to heaven, and waited for the fatal strike.

There was no response from the Almighty.

"Just as I thought," I said in disgust.

Then I took off down the road after my mother.

# Twenty-six

A full moon began to rise that afternoon as we followed the coach road as it snaked through the hills. The sky poured rain for half an hour or so, but there was no thunder or lightning.

The road led steadily down into a thickly wooded hollow, and then we began to climb again. The approach was steeper than the hills we had just traversed, and we could see that the apex, to the southeast, bristled with pines.

"Reckon this must be Pine Mountain," I said.

"I don't see what is so frightening about it," she said. "It looks like every other hill we've walked over in Taney County, and I must say they have an exaggerated opinion of their own terrain if they are going to call *that* a mountain."

But I knew she was anxious because she was walking quickly.

"By the way, I had never better hear you swear as I did behind me on the road a while ago," she said. "I did not know such filth could come from your mouth. I have tried to raise you to be a gentleman, but I see my influence has left you. But that is the order of things when a boy enters his in-between years."

"What do you mean?" I asked.

"Oh, didn't I tell you?" she said brightly. "Happy birthday. You're thirteen now. There was a calendar on the wall of that horrible little store, and that reminded me to check. I meant to tell you back there."

"I turned thirteen," I said.

"Yes," she said.

"And you didn't tell me."

"We lost track of the days on the road," she said. "I knew it was coming, but I did not know that we had spent so much time traveling. I'm sorry, Jacob, but when we get to Springdale we will have some kind of celebration, I promise."

"If it's not my real birthday," I said, "I don't want a party. What will we use for cake and candles, anyway? Zeus's Wounds. We can just wait for next year and celebrate my fourteenth."

"The war will be over by then," she said. "Candles and cake."

"What day is it?"

"It's always been—"

"I know when my birthday is, Mother," I said. "I was referring to today's date, which you saw on the calendar at the store. For weeks I have not known the proper day nor the date, and I would like to because of the notes I keep for myself in the ledger book."

"It's Friday," she said. "The seventh of November."

I stopped, pulled the ledger book from my pocket, and made a note of the date so that I wouldn't forget. Mother was standing by my side, with a hand on my shoulder, but it wasn't until I had closed the ledger and returned it to my pocket that I glanced at my mother and noticed she was staring at something hanging in the tree above.

It was a Federal soldier, strung up by his feet, and his throat had been slit and his belly ripped open. His intestines hung down like a mass of pink sausage dripping blood.

Mother buried her head against my shoulder.

"That confirms it," I said. "Pine Mountain."

"Did you notice something about the dead soldier?" mother asked.

"Quite a bit, actually," I said. "To what do you refer?"

"He is missing his right ear."

"You're right."

Her head stayed on my shoulder.

"Can you tell if it was cut off or chewed off?"

"Chewed off, I'd say."

Mad Jack Vandiver emerged from the brush, threw his head back, and roared with laughter until his face was bright red and tears streamed down his cheeks. He was still dressed in the greasy clothes he had worn at our cabin, and he had a necklace full of fresh ears on his chest.

"It is quite a warning, is it not?" he asked.

"Fit for a pirate," I said.

"Glad you recognized our work," Mad Jack said when he could control his levity enough to speak. "We heard you noting that the ear had been chewed off. Me and my partner take that as quite a compliment."

"Partner?" mother asked.

"The devil, remember?"

"Oh, yes."

Vandiver skipped across the road toward us, swept off his hat, and bowed so low that his long gray hair brushed the ground.

"Pleased to meet you again," he said. "I believe the last time we parted was in the federal prison at Palmyra where you, Eliza Gamble, seemed to have little sympathy for my plight. As I recall, you told me it was my time—but you was *wrong*!"

He convulsed again with laughter.

"What happened?" I asked. "Find somebody willing to *muck* Strachan for you?"

"Oh, no," Mad Jack said enthusiastically. "The devil made special arrangements for my parole. After the rest of the condemned were taken out of the cell, in preparation to be shot, a Yankee jailer came into the cell to make sure that my chains remained secure. I was not one of the ten, but I was to be put down the day after. But this Yankee jailer got too close, and I was able to throw a few links around his windpipe and grind the life right out of him. On his belt I found the keys to the padlocks and the cell, took his cute little revolver, and sent two more Yankee souls to the devil as I was taking my leave."

"Was one of them Strachan?" I asked.

"Oh, almost!" Mad Jack laughed. "I had him lined up good, but he ducked at the last minute, and the ball grazed the top of that big square forehead of his. Was I surprised when he remained on his feet! Alas, my pistol was dry, and I was forced to make a run for it. But it was rather peculiar that I missed my mark, which was the bridge of his patrician nose, and I am suspicious that my partner whispered some little warning to him at the last instant. Oh, what's that?"

Mad Jack listened intently.

"My partner assures me, despite the intercession with the provost marshal, that I remain his favorite."

"Too bad you didn't kill him," I said.

"Well, that was *my* position," Mad Jack said. "But the devil was having none of it."

"That was an amusing story," Mother said. "Now, we will be on our way."

She stepped forward, but two more guerrillas appeared.

"Oh, I'm afraid we can't let you do that," Mad Jack said.

"And why not?"

"You must be brought before the Judgment Tree," Mad Jack said, "so that Alf Bolin can decide your fate. But he is engaged in a little business just now, so we will have to take you to a safe place until he can render his decision."

"Where?"

"Not far," Mad Jack said. "A cabin whose mistress has shown us a little hospitality, and where you can pass the hours in comfort."

"We will do no such thing," Mother said.

"As you wish," Mad Jack said and shrugged. "I have sworn to bring no harm to women, and I will not break that promise now. Sadly, my companions have taken no such vow."

The other guerrillas raised their rifles.

"Stop it," I said. "This is madness."

"Well, the boy has found his voice," Mad Jack said. "When we parted, you were a mousy little thing that was afraid of your own shadow."

"Much has happened," I said.

"I read that in your eyes."

"You know how we have suffered at the hands of the Federals," I said. "They are our common enemy, so let us behave as such. We will submit to this inquisition by this Bolin, as long as you give me your word that no harm will come to my mother."

"She is safe in my care," Mad Jack said, "but I cannot speak for what Bolin will decide."

"Let us go, then," I said.

"I will take your mother to her place of rest," he said, "but you, little man, are going with my companions. I rather think you should see what this Bolin, as you say, is about before you have your hour of judgment."

"No," Mother said. "We stay together."

She drew the Manhattan from her pocket.

Mad Jack held up one hand, indicating that the others should hold their fire.

"Don't be foolish," I told Mother.

I grasped the revolver by the barrel and gently pulled it from her hand. Then I handed it butt-first to Mad Jack, who placed it in his belt.

"I expect that to be returned," I said.

"We shall see," Mad Jack said. "Say, you wouldn't happen to know the day of the week, would you?"

"Of course," I said. "It is Friday."

While Mad Jack led Mother into the woods, the other two walked on either side of me down the coach road and then up the shoulder of Pine Mountain. For all I knew, they were escorting me to my execution.

"Been in this business long?" I asked, striving for

a conversation in hopes of softening their resolve should they be intent upon killing me.

"Since before the war," one said.

"So you were in the fighting along the Kansas border?"

"No," he said. "I mean we have been robbing and killing since before the secession. My brother and I have ranged the White River Valley from here to Arkansas, but have never ventured beyond."

"What do they call you?" I asked.

"Vinegar," the talkative one said. "My brother is Addison."

"Shut up," Addison snapped. "There's no reason to talk."

"Shut up yourself," Vinegar said. "What could it hurt? He's just a kid."

"Kids have big mouths."

"Addy, what's he going to tell that anybody doesn't already know?" Vinegar asked. "There's a Yankee soldier with his guts hanging down in the tree behind us. Are you afraid he will turn opinion against us?"

Despite the grimness of the situation, I laughed.

"How far is Forsyth?" I asked.

"Ten miles or so," Vinegar said. "Why?"

"I understand there is a Federal encampment there," I said. "Why do they allow Bolin to continue to operate?"

"Oh, they've made a few runs against us, but we scatter into the woods and regroup later. The soldiers are unused to such a fight, and give up after a few hours. Every so often, Bolin will catch one of them and hang him from a tree, just to remind them who owns this road."

Then we stopped.

A few dozen yards to the east, on the side of the mountain, was a fortresslike outcropping of gray limestone. Boulders were strewn about its base, and around the rocks lolled the rest of Bolin's cutthroats.

"Which one is he?" I asked.

Vinegar pointed to the top of the highest rock.

Bolin was standing, his rifle in his arms, gazing down into the valley. Then he threw his head back and filled his lungs with the evening air.

"This view," he said, "makes me want to *muck* somebody up."

You already know how Bolin had ambushed the mail coach, burned the wagon, killed one soldier, and obtained the egg-shaped diamond from the other. The corporal knelt before me, his hands clasped, while the lipless one called Scarecrow Jack awaited permission to use his razor on the hapless man.

The navy was extended in my left hand, the muzzle pointed at the man's chest. The hammer was cocked and the chamber beneath it was primed and loaded. My heart pounded in my ears.

"Squeeze the trigger," Bolin urged, "and you will be a child no longer."

I pulled the trigger.

The ball struck the corporal high in the chest, just above his clasped hands and below his throat. He fell on his side, gagging, his hands clutching the wound and his legs flailing wildly.

I cocked the revolver for another shot, but Bolin stopped me.

"Let him choke on his own blood," he said.

Bolin took the revolver from me.

I stepped away, feeling faint. I stumbled and then

went to my knees. On the ground before me was a little mound of a rock, with a hole in the top of it, and through the hole I could see the reflection of the moon.

I plunged my hand into the hollow rock, scooped up some rainwater, and threw it on my burning face.

# Twenty-seven

Bolin sat with his back to the base of a huge oak and drank whiskey from a stoneware jug. His gang sat on logs and rocks scattered in a semicircle around him. Nearby was a fire over which slabs of venison roasted on spits.

I was sitting next to Bolin, my knees drawn up to my chin.

Bolin wiped his mouth with his sleeve and passed me the jug.

"Go ahead," he said. "Drink to your dead Yankee."

The jug was heavy, so I held it in both hands and took a swig. It was the first time I had ever tasted hard liquor, and it burned my mouth and throat, but I tried hard not to show my distress. As I passed the whiskey along, I told myself that I would never try *that* again.

Scarecrow Jack took the jug, pulled down his kerchief, then tilted his head back and poured a long stream into his gaping mouth. Then he replaced the kerchief and passed the jug to the next man.

The gang ate and drank, laughed loudly and

often, and there was much talk about the corporal who had given up the egg-shaped diamond and then pleaded for his life. There was discussion of a campaign to locate the source of the wealth, but Bolin squelched the talk with three words: "After the war."

Along about midnight, Bolin gave a signal, and Addy rolled a stump over to Bolin and set it upright in front of him. Bolin withdrew his large hunting knife and drove it into the heart of the wood.

"Court," he said, "is now in session."

The gang quieted.

"Our first order of business is the young man beside me," Bolin said. "Get to your feet," he told me, "and stand before the bench."

I did.

"Bring the other prisoner."

Mad Jack emerged from the shadows, leading my mother by a rope tied at the waist. Her hands were bound in front. As Mad Jack pulled her beside me, she tossed her head and slung her hair back. She stared at Bolin, her eyes shining in the firelight.

"At the Judgment Tree, we recognize no law save our own and that of nature," Bolin said. "Governments have proven the bane of man, are corrupt without exception, and fill us wholly with contempt. There is no appeal from the verdict of this court. Do you understand?"

"What are we on trial for?" Mother asked.

"Women have no voice here," Bolin said. "If you'd like to ask a question, pass it to your son."

Mother nodded at me.

"What's the charge?" I asked.

"For coming into our territory without cause or

invite," Bolin said. "You, Jacob Gamble, have partially acquitted yourself through action. It is our custom to give prisoners three choices: to join our gang, join the Confederate army, or die. But your mother presents a more difficult problem. Because females cannot be members of the gang or join the rebellion as soldiers, there is but one option."

"Death," I said.

"After they have served our purpose," he said.

"That is unacceptable," I said.

"We are not in the habit of raping the kin of gang members," Bolin said. "And that offers the beginning of a solution. So, I put the first question to you: Will you join our gang, promise to disrespect the laws of the United States, and promise to give your life if needed to protect your fellow gang members, and me in particular?"

"No," Mother said. "He's just a boy."

"Tell the prisoner to be quiet," Bolin said.

"Be still, Mother."

"Further instruct the prisoner that you are thirteen, which is the age of manhood in these hills, and that further you are her only living male relative, which makes her your responsibility, and confers upon you total control."

"This is insane," Mother said. "You're all insane."

Bolin looked at me with expectation.

I stepped in front of Mother, and she attempted to lean around me, to keep eye contact with Bolin. She was furious, continued to protest, and struggled against the rope that Mad Jack held.

"Stop," I said.

"Jacob, don't even consid—"

I struck her face with the back of my hand.

The blow must have been harder than I intended—
or, perhaps, subconsciously I had been waiting for
this moment for a long time—because her head
jerked back, her hair flew forward, and she stumbled
a few steps and nearly went to the ground before Mad
Jack jerked her upright.

"Do you want to die?" I asked her.

Mother dipped her tongue into the blood at the
corner of her mouth and glared at me. She was
panting, her hair was wild, and I think that if her
hands had been free, she would have fought back.
But she looked at me, and then at Bolin, and shook
her head no, that she did not want to die.

"The instructions have been delivered," I said to
Bolin.

It was the only time that I ever struck my mother,
and I am glad for that, and I expect you will be
wanting me to say something along the order that
the blow was necessary, that it was delivered out of
love, and that if I had not done it, we both would
have been dead by morning. That may have been
my deeper reasoning, but the only thing I recall is
being filled with joy at finally having the last word.

"Very well," Bolin said. "Jacob Gamble, what say
you?"

"If I join, my mother will remain unmolested?"

"It is my word," Bolin said. "Any man who violates
the order will answer to me."

"Then I must join," I said.

"You swear?" he asked.

"I swear."

"Then we will proceed with the challenge."

"What challenge?" I asked with alarm.

"Ordinarily, you would have to strip to the waist

and choose one of us to fight, hand to hand, and win," he said. "Then you would have to present me with some kind of tribute to show your gratitude. While tribute is expected, you are at a certain disadvantage when it comes to fighting—you are not quite your mother's equal in height, let alone one of us."

I glanced around me. I may have been able to slap my mother silly while her hands were tied, but I had no chance of besting any of the men who returned my stare.

"Do you propose an alternative challenge?"

"I have been thinking of evening the odds," he said. "Are you fond of riddles?"

"I've never wasted much time on them," I said.

"Too bad for you," Bolin said, "because I have a riddle for you now. If you answer correctly, we will continue. If you don't—well, you know."

"I know."

"Are you ready?"

I nodded.

Bolin leaned forward.

"A cloud was my mother," he recited from memory, "the wind is my father. My son is the cool stream, and my daughter is the fruit of the land. A rainbow is my bed, the earth my final resting place, and I'm the torment of man."

He paused.

"What am I?"

"Oh, that's a good one," Mad Jack said.

"No helping, now," Bolin warned.

I glanced at my mother. Her face was pale with fright and her expression told me that she did not know the answer.

"Repeat it," I said. "Slowly."

He did.

Mother shut her eyes and held her breath, dreading my answer.

"Rain," I said.

Bolin laughed and pounded his fist on the stump.

Mother exhaled.

"Very good," Bolin said. "Now there is only one thing left."

"Tribute," I said.

"That's right," Bolin said. "Show your gratitude."

I ran a hand through my hair and cleared my throat.

"There is nothing I can give you that you do not already possess, or could take if you wanted," I said. "I stand before you with only the clothes on my back and my father's fiddle, which is of value only to me. I'm sure there is one like it in just about every cabin in these hills. But I do have one thing besides, something which I found quite expectedly along the way, and which sparked my childish delight. But as you have pointed out, it is time to give up my childish ways and to join the world of men."

I pulled the little red bullfrog from my pocket and placed it on the stump.

"I don't know who made this figure, or why," I said. "But the mystery is part of its charm, and I would be pleased if you would receive it as a token of gratitude for sparing my life and that of my mother."

Bolin removed the little statue from the stump and ran his fingers over it.

"It is a pipe," he said.

I waited.

"I have plenty of pipes," he said, "but none like this. All it lacks is a stem. Where did you find it?"

"In the mud of a riverbank to the east," I said. "I'm not sure how far."

Bolin placed the bullfrog back on the stump, then removed the egg-shaped diamond from his pocket and placed it in the bowl of the pipe. It fit perfectly.

"Now that," he said, "is the richest damned frog in the world."

The gang roared with laughter.

Bolin stood, plucked the knife from the stump, and walked over to Mother. Her drew her hands forward and severed the rope. His eyes lingered on her just a bit longer than the action required.

"Your promise," I told Mad Jack. "The gun."

He took the Manhattan from his belt and handed it to Bolin, who then handed it to me. I put the gun in the waist of my trousers.

"Fetch your fiddle, boy, and play me a tune to match my mood," Bolin said. "Nothing sad, mind you, no dew-eyed ballad or lament about home across the sea. Do you know anything we can dance to?"

"I believe so," I said as I drew the fiddle from the sack.

I plucked the strings with my thumb, adjusted the pegs a bit, and then tore into the "Eighth of January" as the gang danced madly around the fire.

# Twenty-eight

I became Bolin's aide-de-camp in the weeks to come, with Murder Rock the epicenter of a campaign of unrelenting terror. Yankee soldiers making their way on furlough up the coach road from some lonely post in Arkansas were easy targets, and when the Federals sent a squad of troopers out to catch us, we simply went deeper into the woods. They never followed us very far.

Mother, meanwhile, was directed to stay with Helen Foster, the wife of a Confederate soldier who had been captured and imprisoned in the Federal stockade at Springfield. The cabin was only about three miles south of Murder Rock, hard upon the Arkansas line.

Bolin's habit was to visit the cabin every few days and demand breakfast of Mrs. Foster, but I believe this was just an excuse to be near my mother. I always accompanied Bolin, and while Mother would say nothing in his presence, when she caught me alone she would plead with me to give up my new companions lest I meet an end as gruesome as that of the soldier who had been hanged from a tree when we first approached Murder Rock. These arguments were brief but intense, and each time Mother threatened to walk away on her own, but I knew she would not.

But I could not yet precisely explain why I knew.

I told Mother, with some honesty, that attempting to quit the gang was suicide. Better to spend the winter in Taney County and make a run for it in the spring than to set out unprepared and be hunted down like animals. Besides, Bolin did not require my participation in the killings. Instead, he seemed to relish my company.

Bolin talked about how his mother, Matilda Bolin, had given birth to him during the winter of 1842.[1] He never knew who his father was. His mother repeatedly told him that he was unwanted, that he was the punishment God had visited upon her for having carnal desire, and that the burden of raising him was killing her. When Alf was eleven, his mother ran off with a horse trader and left the boy alone in a one-room cabin on the James River.

After nearly starving to death in the woods, Alf wandered onto a homestead some miles northwest of Forysth and was taken in by the blacksmith and his family there. Their name was Cloud and they already had eleven children, Bolin said, so one more was hardly noticed. They forced Bolin go to school, where he excelled in reading and was the champion speller of his class, but he never became comfortable indoors. He preferred, he

---

1. Most sources give the mother's name as Bolden. Alf, who by all counts was quite literate, deliberately altered the spelling.

said, to spend his time in the woods. He would sometimes be gone for days on end, surviving without gun or knife.

Despite the Cloud family's charity, Bolin never felt any warmth for his adopted family. He took his leave of the clan at the age of seventeen and made his way all the way over to southeastern Missouri, where he became fast friends with a cutthroat by the name of Sam Hildebrand. The outlaw had grown up in a great rock house overlooking Big River and, with his rifle Kill Devil, had become the terror of St. Francois County.

Hildebrand supplied the kind of lessons that Bolin thirsted for, but which could not be found in any country schoolhouse. When the war broke out, Bolin returned to Taney County to start his own gang.

Bolin described his killings to me in exacting detail. He shot David Tittsworth, a boy of sixteen, in the chest while the lad was minding his own business near the old post office on Bear Creek; he forced Old Man Budd to leave his team of oxen and wade into the White River, where he shot the eighty-year-old and left his body to float downstream; along Roark Creek he murdered Young Bill Willis, aged twelve years, as the boy was crossing a rail fence with some field corn for the family horses.

"But why?" I asked Bolin during one of the breakfast visits to the Foster cabin. This was along about Old Christmas, after Marmaduke had made a stab north and routed the Union garrison at Forsyth.[2]

2. Confederate General John S. Marmaduke raided Taney County on Dec. 31, 1861. Old Christmas falls on Jan. 6, and recalls the time before England and her colonies changed from the Julian to the Gregorian calendar in 1752.

"I can understand the soldiers, and the men you rob," I said, "but why kill children and old men? What is to be gained?"

"Target practice," he said.

Helen Foster, who was filling Bolin's cup with coffee when he made the remark, turned pale. Mother, thankfully, did not hear the conversation. She had not yet recovered from the morning sickness she had contracted on the road, and was outside, staining the ground with her vomit.

"I killed Calven Cloud," Bolin said.

"The man that took you in."

Bolin nodded.

"When?" I asked.

Bolin produced the bullfrog and tamped some tobacco into the bowl. He had put the pipe back into use after whittling a stem from a bit of cedar.

"October, I think," he said.

Then he rose from the breakfast table and walked over to the fireplace. The Foster woman kept an old slingblade near the hearth for use in tending the fire, and Bolin picked up the heavy curved thing and used its point to stir the ashes. Then he stooped down, his back to me, and lit the pipe with a glowing ember.

"Why?" I asked.

"Calven was a blacksmith," Bolin said through a cloud of tobacco smoke. "After some minor altercation with some Yankee soldiers, in which I was forced to swim the White River to escape, I found myself in need of a rifle. I knew that Calven had the best rifles in the county, so I elected to pay him a visit and ask him politely for one."

Then Bolin sat in a rocking chair in front of the fire.

"By yourself?"

"Vinegar and Addy were with me," he said. "But we were down to just one old shotgun for all of us. Calven took exception to the fact that I was wearing a hood over my face, and refused to grant my request."

"I've never seen you wear a hood," I said.

Bolin shrugged.

"Seemed like a good idea at the time," he said. "Figured it would make it easier on the old man if he could pretend not to know who I was. But he wasn't playing along. He said he didn't have any weapons, and when I challenged his lie, he told me to take off the hood and ask like a man."

"Did you?"

"I took off my hood," he said, "but I didn't ask. I took the shotgun from Addy and blew Calven's damned head off. Did I mention that he was a Yankee? The sonuvabitch had just joined the Union army."

I walked over to the fireplace and took a straight chair opposite him. But Bolin wasn't looking at me. He didn't seem to be looking at anything in particular.

"Calven's fool of a wife, Mary—"

"—you mean your stepmother."

"Yes, her," Bolin said. "She came out of the house and started screaming and bawling. She kept it up while I took my pick of rifles in the shop. Afterward, I was a bit melancholy. I stopped at a couple of other houses and killed the men I found there, and I felt better straightaway."

"So the rifle you call Lucifer?"

"It was Calven's," he said.

About that time, Mother came in the door, holding

a cloth over her mouth. Bolin brightened at her approach, but Helen Foster scowled.

"How far along are you?" the woman asked.

Mother looked at her in horror.

"What does she mean?" I asked.

"Don't you know?" the woman asked with a wicked smile. "Your mother's with child."

# Twenty-nine

I don't know who took the news harder, me or Bolin. We walked out of the cabin together and, because our mood seemed dark, the rest of the gang—who always stood guard outside the cabin while we ate—backed off and gave us some air.

Bolin walked to the back of the cabin to check the horses, and I followed him. I didn't want to talk, but I didn't want to be alone, either. I figured Bolin would know how it felt for one's mother to be a disappointment.

We had captured the pair from a Union scouting party the week earlier. Bolin had strung one of the dead soldiers in a tree along the coach road, but he'd left the other on the ground, with a message carved into his back: *I found Bolin.*

I touched a hand to the nose of my horse.

"Know those stories about Old Christmas?" I asked, trying to make some conversation. "About how at midnight the animals kneel down and are granted the ability to speak in English, so they might pray—"

"You're asking me about Christmas? I named my rifle Lucifer. Doesn't that give you a hint on where I'd stand on Christmas?" he shouted. "And do you take me for a fool, asking me if I believe the story of animals talking?"

"No, I wasn't asking that," I said.

"Then what?"

"What I was going to ask," I said, "is what do you reckon they'd say if they were granted speech?"

"Animals talk all the time," he said. "Not like humans, but they do. I used to believe I could understand them, but it was just wishful thinking. No creature can really understand another."

Well, I suppose he meant to say "another."

What came out of his mouth was, no creature can really understand *a mother*.

"Who's the father?" he asked.

I shrugged.

"How can you not know?" he asked.

"You mistake my role," I said.

"What have you let her do?" he roared.

"I was a child," I said. "I am a child."

"God damn you," Bolin shouted.

"I'm sure He already has."

"Did you not know that I had—tender feelings— for her?" he screamed. "How could you not know? Who has lain with her? Was it a member of the gang? Name the man and I shall rip his heart beating from his breast."

"I said I don't know."

"You dissemble," he said. "Why?"

He reached out and grasped me by the collar of my coat.

"Do you lie because you have lain with her?"

Then he lifted me from the ground and shook me like a doll.

"No," I protested. "Of course not. I don't know anything about such matters, I've never been with a woman."

"Who, then?"

He shook me again until my teeth rattled.

"A provost marshal in Missouri, perhaps," I said. "Or a rebel soldier who died on the way here."

"The whore!" He threw me aside and I landed on the hard winter ground near the horses, which backed nervously away and strained against their lines. "The putrid whore! Are all women alike? Are all like beasts, driven by the thought of satisfaction of whatever urge they might have at the moment?"

He advanced and shook his finger at me.

"And you, you little pimp," he said. "Even if you didn't lay with her, I'm sure you got something out of the bargain. A roof over your head, a full belly, a little spending money in your pocket?"

I tried to get away, but he had me backed against the rear wall of the cabin. When I lunged one way and then the next, he was so much bigger than me it was like a cat batting at a mouse.

I pulled the Manhattan.

His eyes were all whites, and saliva dripped from his beard. The rest of the gang had run to the rear of the cabin to see what the shouting was, but froze when they saw that Bolin was about to lay on.

"Don't come any closer," I said.

Out of the corner of my eye I saw Mother round the corner of the cabin, her feet flying. Scarecrow Jack reached out and held her tight, a hand clamped over her mouth.

Then Bolin let out a terrible yell and sprang forward.

He kicked the gun out of my hand, and it discharged into the trees as it flew upward. Then he snatched up a rock the size of a melon and struck a glancing blow across my right temple.

That's the last thing I remember about the fight.

When I came to, a couple of days later, I was blind in my right eye. Even though the rock had not touched the organ, the blow had snapped the nerve inside my skull, and the effect was permanent. As time passed, the eye grew milky and was a distraction to others, so I began wearing the patch.

Bolin was scarce for a week after the fight, and I was glad for that. But I have often relived that moment when Bolin kicked the gun from my hand, and pondered about how different things would have been had my shot just been a little quicker.

There are a thousand such moments over a lifetime, of course, each of which we ruminate upon and curse ourselves either for our action or lack of action. The frightening thing is that we only know a fraction of those moments, for most of the time we are blissfully unaware of the wheel of fate. But regret digs deepest when we have only ourselves to blame.

I made a point never to complain about my injury, and Mother seemed to bear far more weight from it than I. She pressed me again about leaving, and I told her that it would be soon. We would slip away with the horses at the first good chance that presented itself, I promised.

Then I took leave of the cabin for a few days.

I went to Kirbyville, where we had spied the taverns,

and spent some of my stolen money on the whores
there. Nobody knew me, and nobody cared as long as
I had coin. It was Bolin they wanted. And yes, I could
have turned Bolin in at that point, but that would
have put my mother in jeopardy.

I know you expect me to say the whores didn't
help, that my emptiness grew afterward, but that
was only true for the first time. Things began to
pick up afterward. By the time I returned to the
cabin, I can't say that it made much difference in
the long run, but I was glad to know what all the
fuss was about.

When Bolin came back, after having taken the
gang on a spree of murder and pillage across the
Arkansas line, he did not speak of the incident. He
treated me as he had before, and if I had not lost
the eye, I would have had no proof that we had ever
had a cross word.

# Thirty

A fortnight later, we were back at Murder Rock.

It wasn't that we were expecting to find much on the coach road that day. Traffic had dwindled to nothing, either from fear of Bolin or because the winter had struck the Ozarks with a vengeance. It had been below freezing for several days, the leaves were long gone from the trees, and icicles hung from the bare branches. But Bolin did not like to be holed up inside for any length of time, so he once again took the gang out to the rock, more out of boredom than anything else.

Bolin and I sat atop the rock while the rest of the gang was below. Vinegar had started a small fire on the ground in the fissure between the largest and the lower rock, which gave considerable warmth because it had two hard surfaces to radiate from. Most of the gang was squeezed down there, their backs against the rocks and their feet propped up on logs, and Vinegar had taken an old canvas and stretched it between the rocks, making a rough but serviceable shelter.

Some of the boys were cleaning their guns, others were drinking for entertainment and to fortify themselves against the cold, and Mad Jack had a card game going on the top of a powder barrel. Vinegar and Addy and Scarecrow Jack were clustered around the card game, and they were playing poker for some of the loot that we had taken from our victims over the winter. In addition to gold and silver coins, there were rings and watches and fobs, and an assortment of utilitarian items that were of more value in the wilderness than the conventional riches: There were canteens, cartridge boxes, shaving kits, combs, soap, candles, tins of percussion caps, powder flasks, patent medicines, blankets, gloves, shoes, boots, and so forth.

As darkness came, bayonets were driven into porous sides of the rock and candles were mounted in the hafts, giving a little light for the men to gamble by. Their appearance was beginning to look a little less like pirates than soldiers whose uniforms were drawn from a motley collection of both blue and gray. Some of them, such as Addy, had taken to wearing cavalry swords, even though he had no horse. Even I had played a few hands with Mad Jack, and had come away with a pair of gloves and an old black slouch hat.

I climbed back on top of the rock and sat down next to Bolin, who was busy skinning a fox he had shot earlier in the day. He was deft with his knife, and soon had cut the fox's head and cape away from the rest of the body, and when he placed this cap over his head, he looked even more feral.

"What do you think?" he asked.

"You should have tanned that first," I said. "You look like a lunatic."

"That's what I was aiming for," he said. "But I can't say that hat makes you look any more fierce."

"Wasn't trying for fierce," I said. "I was trying for warmth. If you hadn't noticed, it's freezing."

"The weather don't bother me none," he said. He was still wearing the buckskins that had become his trademark, and he had no coat. "I've learned to deal with the cold. Instead of fighting it, you just need to become a part of it, to let it blow through you like it does the branches of the trees. It's thinking about it that makes folks miserable. You'll learn."

"The business at the Judgment Tree," I said. "I know where you get that. Daniel Boone, when he was the Spanish syndic along the Mississippi."

"Well, I reckon I'm the biggest syndic here," he said. "But I sure as hell ain't no Dan'l Boone."

Bolin had a handful of teeth that he had pried from the jawbone of the fox cupped in his hand. He placed them in the bed-ticking patch and poured them down the barrel of Lucifer and tamped them down with the ramrod.

"What do you suppose these'll do to somebody?"

"Don't know," I said. "They could just be blown to dust."

"Or they could come out of the barrel like shards of glass."

"That sounds fairly ugly."

"Should be," Bolin said, and smiled.

Then he balanced Lucifer across his knees and peered at me from beneath the fox head. His gaze made me a bit uncomfortable.

"Well, Lieutenant," he said, "What do you think? Should we quit the rock for the night or hang on just a little longer?"

To keep from looking at him, I gazed upward. There was a blanket of stars beyond the tree branches.

"The cold is a benefit if you're driving a wagon," I said. "The ground has firmed up, there are no mud holes to bog down in, and making a run at night might seem to be an advantage, since all of our ambushes have taken place from dawn to dusk. They might figure it's so cold that we're holed up in our caves and cabins for the night. But who knows? These are Yankees. I don't pretend to understand them."

"The rock is lit up like a Christmas tree," Bolin said. "Nobody is going to come down the road tonight."

"Unless they wanted to find us," I said. "In that case, we've announced ourselves."

Bolin laughed.

"Who would challenge us?" he asked. "Every bluebelly in southwest Missouri soils his pants just at the mention of the name of Alf Bolin."

"I'm sure you're right," I said.

Bolin reached into his pocket and withdrew a bottle of whiskey. He uncorked it, took a long pull, and offered it to me. To his surprise, I took it from him and had a long swallow myself.

"Been studying bad habits, eh?"

"That and more," I said.

"How you getting along with that damned patch?"

"Thought we had silently agreed not to talk about that," I said.

I took another drink and handed the bottle back.

"We can talk," he said. "This once."

"What was your intent?" I asked.

"When?"

"You know when."

"My intent was to kill you," he said. "I felt betrayed."

"You are the smartest person I know, and you're certainly the strongest. You knew that I was no match for you. What happens in that mind of yours?"

"I don't know," he said, and slipped the bottle back in the pocket of his shirt. "I am sometimes seized by a kind of fit, in which I cannot think and can barely see, and all I feel is rage. Ever hear of the old Norse berserkers? Well, it's like that. Letting blood is the only thing that relieves the condition."

"I thought we were friends."

"We are," Bolin said. "But that won't save you from another one of my fits, if I throw my rage in your direction. If that happens, I want you to run like hell and stay away for a spell until I come to my senses."

"You could have told me that before you bounced a rock off my head. I was rather fond of my right eye."

Bolin looked away. If he was sorry, he wouldn't say so.

"So, the patch," he said. "Does it hamper you?"

"I forget about it, most of the time, until I have to try to judge distance. But I am left-handed and left-eyed, so my shooting has not suffered. I am at a disadvantage from someone coming up on my right side, however. My brain has compensated so that it seems like I have a full field of vision, but I have to tilt my head to the right to get a field that's not skewed to the left."

"You nearly killed me," he said. "You came closer than anyone else ever has. I saw the barrel of the nasty little pistol pointed true at me, and I just kicked instinctively. Had I missed that kick, you would be leading the gang now."

"And have a four-thousand-dollar reward on my head? No, thank you. Nobody can fill your shoes. If somebody is lucky enough to get close enough to put you down, the rest of the gang will just drift away."

Bolin sighed.

"What has made you the way you are?" I asked.

"I've told you the story of my childhood."

"There must be more," I said. "Plenty of folks get abandoned as children, but they manage to grow up without becoming master murderers."

Bolin looked downcast.

"What is it?" I asked.

"My mother," he said. "When she was drunk—and she was drunk most of the time—she did unnatural things with me."

"You mean like witchcraft?"

"Damn, but you are green in the damnedest ways," he said. "No, she wasn't a witch. Just a poor old drunk who wanted her precocious son to take the role of an absent father. I suppose she was driven to in an attempt to relieve her loneliness."

"How sad," I said.

"And terrible," Bolin said, "at least when she abandoned me in favor of the horse trader. I was too young to know that there was anything wrong with it. After all, I had spent my entire life up to then in that one-room cabin with her. Later, when the Cloud family took me in, I didn't even know enough to keep my mouth shut. Old Calven and his wife were horrified. They said I was an animal, that I was possessed of the devil, and they prayed over me constantly. Of a sudden, I was filled with a shame I had never known. So, when I struck out on my own, I decided to wholly embrace animal ways. Those that now call me an animal mean it as a slur, but from my point of view, it is a high compliment."

Then Bolin's eyes narrowed and he tilted his head a bit. From far down the road to the north came the sound of wheels rumbling down the frozen ruts.

The gang heard it, too.

"What's your pleasure?" Addy called from below.

"Blood is my pleasure," Bolin said. "Prepare your-selves for mayhem."

"Should we douse the fire?"

"No," Bolin said. "Leave it, and the tallows. Seeing the rock all lit up should scare the hell out of 'em."

A farm wagon rolled down the road. A lone soldier was in the driver's seat, and he circled the team around and reined them to a stop at the base of the rock. The man was young, in his late teens perhaps, and the sleeves of his uniform had but a single chevron—a lowly private. He set the brake and threw down the reins, then stood and shouted at the rock.

"Alf Bolin!" he called.

Vinegar lowered his rifle over the top of a boulder and cocked the hammer.

"Want I should kill him?"

"No," Bolin said, just loud enough for the gang to hear.

"Bolin!" the soldier shouted again. "I know your gang has a dozen rifles trained on me, and my life may be forfeit, but I'm willing to take that risk in order to find the man that butchered my father."

"What he lacks in brains he makes up for in nerve," Bolin muttered. "It's Peter, the idiot son of Calven Cloud." Then he stood, cradling Lucifer, and his figure was illuminated by the fire below.

"You've found me," Bolin called. "Now, what do you intend to do with me?"

"Come down here," Cloud said. "And we shall discuss it."

"I have always enjoyed the advantage of height over you, Peter, and I am reluctant to yield it now," Bolin called.

"Whatever advantage you may enjoy in this world, you will surely lose in the next," Cloud said. "But I won't be delayed—I will take my vengeance now. And I will take my father's gun back."

"Smells like a trap," Vinegar said nervously. "There could be fifty Yankees out there in the darkness."

"I come alone," Cloud said.

"Why the wagon?" Bolin asked. "What have you in the bed and why did you pull it back around to the north"

"There is nothing in the back, yet," Cloud said. "But I intend to haul your body back to Springfield in it."

"Let me chew his ears off," Mad Jack offered.

"No," Bolin said.

"Will you come down?" Cloud asked.

"After I am satisfied that you are alone," he said.

Then he called for Vinegar, Addy, and Scarecrow to discharge their rifles into the air. They did, and the volley echoed from the distant hillside.

No trap was sprung.

"Well?" Cloud asked.

Bolin scrambled down from the rock and I followed.

Cloud jumped down from the wagon.

"Name your weapon," Cloud said.

"Teeth," Bolin said. He was about twenty yards away from Cloud, and he brought Lucifer to his hip and fired. The load of fox teeth peppered the soldier, cutting his hands and face, but did no serious damage.

Cloud touched his cheek, examining the blood on his fingertips.

"I should have expected no better," he said.

Bolin laughed. He threw Lucifer to Mad Jack, who caught the rifle with one hand. Then he tossed his knife aside and pulled his shirt over his head. He wadded the shirt into a ball and tossed it behind him.

Never again have I seen a man like Bolin. His muscles rippled beneath his skin like those of a horse, the tendons in his neck were as thick as rope, and his clenched fists resembled mallets.

"Your weapon?" Cloud asked.

"I am my own weapon," Bolin said, then advanced.

As the distance between them closed, Bolin seemed like Goliath in comparison. But Cloud was no David—instead of trying to outsmart Bolin, he assumed a prizefighter's stance and prepared to trade blows.

But Bolin had another plan.

Instead of standing toe-to-toe with Cloud, Bolin put his head down and drove his shoulder into the man's stomach. The force of the assault lifted Cloud from his feet and deposited him flat on his back, gasping for air.

"Having trouble catching your breath?" Bolin asked, and then drove the toe of his boot into Cloud's ribs.

Cloud flinched with pain, but caught Bolin's foot in his hands. He twisted the foot to an unnatural angle and now Bolin went down.

"I'm going to pull your guts out and feed them to you," Bolin said as he got to his feet. Then he advanced again on Cloud, and even though the young man tried to kick him away, Bolin reached down with his right hand, clutched him by the front of his jacket, and pulled him close.

Cloud drove his knee into Bolin's groin, to no apparent effect.

"Sorry," Bolin said. "Those are made of stone."

Then Cloud drew back and struck Bolin in the jaw with his right hand, putting everything he had left into the blow. Bolin looked surprised and sagged a bit, but kept the front of Cloud's uniform blouse firmly clenched in his right hand.

Cloud's eyes burned with hate.

He spat in Bolin's face.

Then Bolin lifted Cloud, held him above his head for a few seconds, and tossed him. The young man landed on the ground, rolled a few feet, and let out a low moan.

"This is what you call vengeance?" Bolin shouted.

Cloud had turned and was trying to crawl away,

but Bolin walked over and grasped the man's ankle and pulled him back. Then he drove a right fist into Cloud's back, over his kidney, and the soldier let out a pitiful cry.

"Your fury should know no bounds," Bolin said as he kicked Cloud again. "Your hatred should drive you to feats of inhuman strength and animal cunning. The image of your dead father, crying for blood, should make your soul thirst for my murder. And yet, you cower before me like a dog!"

Then Cloud spied the knife that Bolin had thrown on the ground before the fight, and his right hand shot out for it. But just as his fingers closed over the handle, Bolin's boot came down on his forearm.

I could hear the bones snap like kindling.

"Oh," Mad Jack said, "that was a good one. He's done for, now. Let me chew his ears off."

"When he's dead," Bolin said.

"Aw, that ain't no fun," Mad Jack said. "I likes to see 'em squirm."

Cloud writhed on the ground, clutching his broken arm to his chest. His face was drawn up into a terrible grimace, his teeth flashing in the firelight, blood trickling down the corner of his mouth.

Bolin stood over him, sweat glistening from his arms and chest, and wiped his mouth with the back of his hand. It came away bloody.

"A lucky shot," Bolin said. "But I have to admit, the boy knows how to punch."

"Are you going to pull his guts out now?" Vinegar asked.

Bolin looked at the young man on the ground. Suddenly, his eyes softened.

"Years ago," he said, "Peter showed me some little kindness. I was eleven or perhaps twelve years old, we were going to school together, and we shared the same desk. It was my first time in a real school, and I was uncomfortable, and the schoolmistress was suspicious of me. She asked me a number of rude questions, as clannish folk are want to do—who was my father, where was my mother, why was I living with the Cloud family?"

Bolin paused.

"I remained silent, ashamed, but Peter spoke up. He did not say that my mother had run off with a horse trader or that I did not know my father's name. Rather, he said that I had been orphaned by some wicked disease that had taken both of my parents. From that moment on, the schoolmistress was a little softer on me, and for the first time I felt accepted. As time passed, I discovered a talent for letters. Even though I'm sure the schoolmistress later learned the truth, she never mentioned it."

The young soldier groaned and tried to rise, but fell back. In addition to his broken arm, he undoubtedly had broken ribs, a bruised if not burst kidney, and a fractured jaw. With some luck, if he was not bleeding too badly inside and infection did not set in, he might live.

Bolin picked him up, carried him to the wagon, and laid him in the bed. I was relieved. It was the first time I had ever seen Bolin extend any kindness.

"Addy," he said. "Kill him."

"That's no fun," Mad Jack said. "Let's split his ribs in back and jerk his lungs out, and watch them flap like a bird's wings until he dies."

"That's a good idea," Scarecrow Jack mumbled

from beneath the kerchief that hid his face. "I've never seen that before, but I'd like to try it."

"He's earned a quick death," Bolin said. "We'll send the wagon back up the road as a message to the Yankees."

Addy began to climb down from the second tier of rocks with his single-barreled shotgun.

"Let me do it," I said quickly.

Bolin stared at me.

"I haven't killed a Yankee since that first night," I said. "I'm anxious to send another one to hell."

I drew the Manhattan.

"Do what you will," Bolin said, and walked toward the rock.

Leaning over the side of the wagon, I pointed the revolver at the young soldier's head. His eyes were open, and he watched as I drew the hammer back with my thumb.

"Make no sound," I whispered.

Then I aimed as near his head as I dared, to make it look convincing, and fired. I turned my head away, as if disgusted by the gore.

Then I went to the front of the wagon, released the brake, and shouted and fired the Manhattan into the air. The team bolted and took the wagon back down the coach road toward the Federal camp at Forsyth.

# Thirty-one

Toward the end of January, Helen Foster took in a sick Confederate soldier who had been paroled and was attempting to make his way back home to Fort Smith. Bolin had asked to see the soldier that day, but the woman had explained that the man had pneumonia and was too ill to come down from the loft.

We returned three days later, and Bolin said it was time to meet the soldier. When the Foster woman objected that the man was still too weak to descend the stairs, Bolin carried Lucifer to the bottom of the ladder and shouted that he'd damn well better find some strength, or else he would come up and put a ball in his brain to end his misery.

The man coughed, but said he would be down directly.

Mother and I were sitting at the table, fairly miserable with one another. We had long since stopped arguing with one another and had settled instead for a dreadful silence. It was coming up on five months since the night at Palmyra, and her belly had started to swell.

The rebel soldier slowly made his way down the ladder, a blanket spread over his shoulders. His uniform was ragged, but he did not look as thin as the other rebel soldiers we had seen on the road. He was thirty or younger, and he had a full head of yellow hair and a beard to match.

"What's your name?" Bolin asked.

"Thomas," the man said. "I'm grateful for your protection."

Bolin offered his hand, and the men shook.

Helen Foster was preparing the evening meal, and it seemed to me that she was more reserved than usual. Typically, she never let a conversation go by without injecting her own little opinion into it, but on this evening she tended to her cooking and seemed unwilling to engage in conversation, even when invited.

"Your color is good," Bolin said. "How do you feel?"

"Better," Thomas said.

"Think you'll be able to travel soon?"

"I expect so," Thomas said. "The sooner I get to Fort Smith, the better."

"A warm home waiting, eh?" Bolin asked. "Wife, children?"

"Yes," the man said. "Three. Children, not wives."

Bolin laughed.

Then Foster set the table and the four of us ate some damned meal that consisted of lots of corn and precious little meat. Bolin, who sat with his back to the wall and Lucifer near at hand, asked Thomas a few questions about life in the rebel

army, and the man said it consisted of much
drilling and very little action, at least up until the
time he had been captured during some skirmish
in Greene County.

After dinner, Bolin went to a rocking chair near
the fireplace and asked me and Thomas to join
him. He left Lucifer resting against the wall. I was
glad of the opportunity to get a little distance between myself and my mother, who was helping the
Foster woman clean up.

Bolin produced the bullfrog pipe and filled it
with tobacco.

"What are you so melancholy about?" he asked me.

"Nothing," I said. "Everything."

I took a seat on the floor, since the men had
taken the only chairs near the fireplace.

"Get up and let my Jacob sit there," Bolin told the
man.

"No, it's all right," I said. "He's sick and should be
closest to the fire."

Bolin left the chair and stooped before the fireplace, seeking a live coal with which to light his
pipe.

Then Thomas picked up the slingblade resting
on the hearth and, while Bolin was still kneeling
with his head turned, brought the blade down with
all of his strength.

The heavy blade made an ugly sound as it buried
itself in Bolin's skull. Bolin dropped the bullfrog
pipe and toppled into the fireplace.

It had happened too fast for me to draw the Manhattan or even shout a warning to Bolin.

Then I drew my gun as Thomas and I looked at
each other in mutual horror. I cocked the revolver

and was prepared to kill the murderer when Bolin lifted himself from the hearth, his arms outstretched, bellowing his rage.

His hair and beard had been singed, and the tip of his nose was black.

From the front side, it was apparent that the blade had sunk all the way to Bolin's heavy brow, and the tip of the blade protruded from his forehead like a metal horn of a new-fashioned demon. Deep in the fissure, you could see bits of white bone and glistening gray matter. He was bleeding heavily from the nose and mouth, and stumbling about the cabin as if drunk.

Thomas grasped the haft of the blade with both hands, wrenched it out of Bolin's skull, and struck him again with it. This time, the blade hit his neck and went deep into the shoulder. Thomas withdrew the blade yet once more and, with Bolin still on his feet and looking squarely at him, used a sideways thrust that caved in the top of Bolin's skull.

Bolin's feet went out from beneath him and he landed with a crash on the plank floor. Bolin was trying to say something, but Thomas could not understand him.

"He shouldn't still be breathing," Thomas said.

I bent down, and Bolin managed a smile.

With great effort, he formed two words: "Kill me."

I knelt. I kissed Bolin on his grisly forehead, and then placed the Manhattan at the base of his skull and pulled the trigger. Bolin's body jerked for a few brief seconds, and then was still.

"You're not sharing in the reward," Thomas said.

"That is what this is about?" I asked. "Money"

"The Federal commander at Springfield has

offered four thousand dollars for proof that Bolin is no longer," Thomas said. "I reckon the head ought to be the best proof of that."

"Why hell, you nearly cleaved his head right off his shoulders with that blade," I said. "Might as well get an ax and finish the job, as long as there's four thousand dollars gold at stake. I just want you to understand that I want none of it. None of it, do you see?"

Thomas was Zachariah E. Thomas, a Union trooper from Iowa, who had been sent to kill Bolin.[1] He was aided by the Foster woman, who had been promised the release of her husband Robert from the stockade at Springfield.

"It's time," Mother said. "Let us make for the horses. If we wait here, we might end up on the floor with our heads separated from their bodies."

"I swore to protect him," I said.

"Nobody could have protected Bolin from himself," she said. "Come on, Jacob, let's go."

I handed the Manhattan to Mother and then raced over to near the fireplace, where I found the bullfrog pipe. I stuffed it into my pocket. Thomas and Helen Foster had concluded that the best way to decapitate Bolin was to saw his head off, and they had placed him on the table where we had eaten dinner and were preparing a crosscut saw for the job.

I leaned over the table and hugged Bolin's barrel chest.

---

1. Gamble makes it seem that Thomas came all the way from Iowa. But the 19th Iowa Infantry was garrisoned at Forsyth in February 1863, and it seems reasonable to conclude that he was a member of the unit. It is unclear from the historical record, however, if the reward was ever paid.

"It's not your fault, Alf," I said, crying. "Your mother just couldn't do any better. If you'd had a mother that loved you, you wouldn't have been a monster. You'd be teaching kids in these hills how to hunt and fish, to spell and solve riddles."

Then I reached into his pocket and withdrew the robin's-egg diamond, but kept it hidden in the palm of my hand. Still sniffling, I slipped the rough gem into my coat and joined my mother outside.

The gang had fled, every one of them—even Mad Jack.

Mother handed me the Manhattan and I mounted Bolin's horse while she took mine, and we rode down to the coach road.

I paused at the base of Murder Rock and placed the red bullfrog at the bottom of the little chimney that always had water, then scooped in a few other stones to cover it up. I didn't want anybody to ever have Bolin's bullfrog pipe, but I wanted to know where it was so that I could think of it and feel good.

Then I got back on the horse and Mother and I took the coach road south, and once we hit the Arkansas line, we just kept going right on through until we hit the Red River in Texas.

The date was February 1, 1863.

They buried Bolin's body in an unmarked grave along the bank of Swan Creek, a mile north and some east of Forsyth. Then they took his head to Ozark, where they stuck it on a pike and paraded it around the courthouse square while the townsfolk jeered and children threw rocks at it. This was a scene more fit for the Middle Ages than the middle of the nineteenth century.

Then Mary Cloud, who was seven months pregnant, was summoned in freezing weather to identify her adopted child and the man who had killed her husband and forty to sixty others in and around Taney County.

The head was left on the pike in front of the courthouse for weeks, until a storm finally blew it down. When last seen, it was being rooted down the muddy street by a pack of hogs.

A Yankee soldier by the name of Benjamin McIntyre was at Forsyth the day that Bolin's body was brought into camp, and he recorded the event in his diary. Turns out that this soldier, who had played no part in Bolin's capture and who has since been lost to history, had the last word on Alf Bolin.

"He was a large sinewy man and must have been of great strength and endurance," McIntyre wrote. "His hair was matted with blood and clotted over his face, rendering him an object of disgust and horror. Today hundreds gloat over his unnatural corpse and exult that his prowess is at an end. . . . *Thus perished a monster.*"

# Thirty-two

Four months later, in the summer of 1863, in a shabby rented room at Sherman, Texas, Mother gave birth to a boy. A midwife had delivered the child, but when she was unable to staunch the flow of blood after, she summoned a quite drunk surgeon who was attending to the needs of a nearby encampment of rebel irregulars.

He sobered a bit after examining Mother.

"Your sister," he said, "is going to die."

"It's my mother," I said.

The surgeon shook his head while wiping his hands on his apron, which was stained with the dried blood of dozens of previous patients.

"Is there nothing you can do?" I asked.

"Say your good-byes," the surgeon suggested as he placed a bloody hand on my shoulder.

He left me alone with Mother, and I held her hand and spoke to her in reassuring tones. I told her how much I had enjoyed growing up on the farm in Shelby County, being cared for by both Mother and Father, and learning to play the fiddle a bit. Then she rallied somewhat and her eyes opened, and I spoke to the point.

"I'm sorry for leading a wicked life," I said. "It would have been better if Bolin had blinded me altogether, instead of allowing me only half the light. I'm especially sorry for the time that I struck you, and I pray for your forgiveness."

She managed a smile.

"Mother," I said. "What am I to do without you?"

She motioned for me to lean down close.

"I have," she said with difficulty, "always cared for you. Before all else. Even your father."

I began to weep.

She asked me not to cry, but to play instead.

I took up the fiddle and played "Star of the County Down" for her until she was gone. Then I sat beside her and gently closed her eyes.

Then I closed mine, placed my head in my hands, and cried until my cheeks were damp and snot frothed in my nostrils.

The surgeon came back in a little while.

"I'm sorry, son, but it happens," he said. "I've made arrangements with the undertaker here. Can you pay?"

I nodded. I had sold the egg-shaped diamond for a song, but it proved enough to get by.

"That's good, makes things easier," he said. "You have a healthy brother—"

"Half-brother," I corrected him.

"All right, a healthy half-brother in there giving his lungs a try, and you need to hire him a wet nurse until he can eat solid food. You have money for that?"

I nodded.

"Good," he said. "There's just one last thing you have to do."

The doctor produced a pad and pencil from his bag and began to fill out the certificate of birth.

"What's that?" I asked.

"Name him," he said.

I put my head down and listened to the hungry little bastard scream.

"Did your mother give you any clue?" the doctor asked.

"No," I said.

"Would it be appropriate to name him after the father—"

"I never knew his name," I said.

"All right, then it's up to you. Choose."

"His name is Ishmael," I said.

Twenty years later he and I would fight it out in Cochise County, Arizona Territory. But it is too early in the morning now for that story.

# Thirty-three

It was dawn. Huston and his young friend had left shortly after the electricity was restored—but not before pressing a note into my hand with a Los Angeles address—and Gamble and I had talked the night away.

The House of Lords was deserted now, and long since closed, but the owner had let us stay. Dorizzi had seen me plenty of times, and knew I worked just across the alley at the newspaper. He told me to leave by the back entrance when we were done, and to make sure the door locked behind us.

Light was streaming in though the windows, and Gamble peered out the window at Main Street. The only thing moving was a milk wagon.

He appeared old now.

"That's it?" I asked.

"Almost," he said. "You have all there is to know about me, for at thirteen my life was cast. You can guess the rest."

I gathered my notes and shoved myself away from

the table. There was more I wanted to ask him. What was it like being chased by the Pinkertons after the war, for example, and what happened when he and his half-brother Ishmael finally squared off in the Arizona desert? The whole bloody thing was equal parts Bible story and Greek tragedy.

But I was exhausted and, in a few hours, I'd have to be at work.

"I'd like to continue this conversation sometime," I said.

"You'd better hurry," Gamble said. "I've lived my threescore and ten, and then some."

"I'm not worried."

"Well, I am," he said. "Somebody might kill me."

He stood and stretched. "You know, if I were just a bit younger . . ."

The years seemed to roll away once again.

"I know," I said. "But I'm not the marrying kind."

"Shame," Gamble said.

We walked toward the stairs.

"Damn, I almost forgot," I said.

I went to the bar, reached behind it, and withdrew the sack I had left there with Dorizzi when I stood at the bar the night before, sizing Gamble up.

"What's this?" he asked.

"Consideration," I said, and handed him the flour sack.

He opened it and withdrew the fiddle. The strings and the bridge were gone, the scroll was chipped, and the finish was dark and checkered with age.

He ran his finger over the body, lingering on the curves.

"It looks," he said, "the way I feel."

"Thought you might want it back."

"Where did you find this?" he asked.

"My friend at the penitentiary. You seemed to be in a bit of a hurry when you departed Jefferson City, and he said you left this behind."

"You didn't—"

"Tell him that I had actually heard from you? No. But I said I wanted to borrow it to write my story about the fiddling outlaw. Said I'd return it. But things have a way of getting lost in the mail these days."

"Thank you," he said.

"You could probably get a pardon after all this time," I suggested. "I could help with the governor, if you want. There's a Democrat in office now. New Deal and all that. And it could be a popular thing, since everybody in Missouri seems to claim some rebel blood now."

His face turned dark.

"I'll ask no pardon," he said. "If there's one thing I can't stand, it's a hypocrite."

We left the bar, making sure the door locked behind us, and walked down the fire escape into the alley. He tucked the fiddle beneath his right arm and held out his left hand to me.

"I know, it seems kind of backwards," he said. "But this is the only way it feels natural."

Rather awkwardly, I shook his hand.

Then I had to ask one last question.

"Did you ever have your chance with Strachan?"

# Epilogue

Late one evening, in 1881, I was in St. Louis with some cash in my pocket, after having pulled some small job down in the Missouri boot heel, and was leaving a brothel on Sixth Street when I noticed an old man coming my way up the sidewalk.

There was something familiar about the man, and I knelt on the bricks beneath a street lamp and pretended to tie one of my shoelaces in order to get a better look. The man was near sixty, walked with a limp, but his features were unmistakable. His hair was still long, although now shot with gray. Above his left eye was an old scar where a pistol ball had left a furrow back to the hairline.

"Strachan," I said.

The man stopped.

He was wearing one of those silly business suits that were fashionable at the time, all cuffs and lapels, and he seemed to be preoccupied with his errand.

"Do I know you?"

I stood and smiled easily.

"We met once," I said. "I was just a boy, but I've never forgotten it."

"I'm sorry, but I don't remember," Strachan said.

"Oh, that's to be expected," I said. "It was a long time ago, during the war, when you were the provost marshal at Palmyra. I expect you remember my mother, though. Her name was Eliza Gamble."

"I don't recall," he said.

He tried to move on, but I placed a firm hand on his arm.

"She was twenty-six," I said. "Pretty. Auburn hair and blue eyes. Came to your office one night in October wearing a man's butternut coat with a .36-caliber Manhattan revolver in the pocket. But you wouldn't have known about the gun, because she never drew it."

"Nonsense."

But his eyes told me that he remembered.

"She came to plead for the life of my father," I said.

Fear crossed his face like the shadow of a bird, then was gone. He drew himself up to his full height and the demeanor I remember so well returned.

"I see the apple has not fallen far from tree," he said. "You come from a family of white trash and I see that you are content to wallow in the gutter as well. I have powerful friends here, and one word from me would land you in the city jail for quite a long time."

He jerked his arm away.

"At least I'm an honest thief," I said. "You stole from your friends and neighbors, you had them killed when it suited you, and you did it all under the color of law."

He smiled, and it was as wicked as I remembered it. "Son, you forget," he said. "My side won the war." Then he laughed.

"What happened to your eye?" he asked. "Did you run with scissors?"

"It's peculiar, you know," I said, moving close to him. "Funny really, in a way. Everything about you that I hated most I became. You had more of an influence on me than my own father. I drink, I smoke cigars, and I take the things I want by threat of violence, backed by a willingness to use it. The first thing I ever felt passionately about in my life was to feel a gun in my hand, that gun my mother had in her coat, and to know what it would feel like to use it on you. Since that day in Palmyra, I have recreated the events over and again in my mind, and my preference in women has always been for those who resemble my mother. So you might say I have spent my life fantasizing about killing you and fucking my mother."

He looked down at the Manhattan, which I had drawn from inside my coat. The revolver had been modified to accept .38 cartridges a few years earlier. The loading lever had been removed, the cylinder had been rechambered, and a thumb port had been added on the left side to ease loading and ejection. We were close enough that the barrel brushed against the fabric of his vest.

"Why don't you, then?"

"Because that would be too good for you," I said. "And it would be too easy for me. You're old, you're unarmed save for your arrogance, and now I realize it wouldn't fix any of the things I once believed it might."

He glanced down and studied the gun.

"So you have kept this antique for this one purpose?"

"One among many," I said.

"Clever," he said. "The ejection gate is on the left side, to match your eye and your hand."

I put the gun back inside my coat.

"Oh, there is one last thing you should know," I said. "My mother died giving birth to your bastard. His name is Ishmael and he is nineteen now, off somewhere in Texas and raising hell. He is wilder than I am and has not yet learned restraint."

"Why should I care?" Strachan sneered.

"Because he has sworn to kill you as well," I said. "Now that I know where you are, I will get word to him. Ordinarily, we don't speak, but blood is thicker than water in these matters. You are old, but have a decade or more of life left. That is quite a lot of time to sit and wonder just when the fatal blow will come."

He backed away, his eyes wide.

"On behalf of my mother," I said, "I bid you good night."

# Afterword

Seventy years and more have passed since Frankie Donovan interviewed Jacob Gamble at the House of Lords. The bar, which was among the most famous west of the Mississippi, closed its doors for good in 1956.

No prints of *Hellfire Canyon* exist. After poor box office following the Joplin premiere, all reels in circulation were recalled by the studio and placed in storage, along with the masters, in a shed at the RKO lot in Culver City, California.

David O. Selznick rented the lot from RKO to make his 1939 masterpiece, *Gone with the Wind,* and the shed was accidentally consumed by fire during the burning of Atlanta. A memo at the time, noting the destruction of the shed, stated that nothing of value had been lost.

Donovan's byline disappeared from the newspaper late in 1934.

The only clue to her departure was a yellowed job application, discovered at the bottom of a metal file cabinet in the newspaper's archive. It was placed, either by mistake or by some now unfathomable logic, in an envelope containing a clipping (by someone else) about the Barrow Gang's 1933 escape after the police had them cornered in a garage apartment in south Joplin.

Donovan had completed the single-page application in pencil, and had listed her birthplace as Chicago. She had attended Northwestern University, but had not graduated. She was unmarried, and had listed her Joplin address as a boarding-house on Seventh Street. Now, there's a convenience store at that location.

An editor had noted, in ink, significant events: hired as classified girl in January 1930; made reporter in 1931; and finally, *left for California*, with no date given.

Murder Rock remains in Taney County, and has so far escaped the destruction wrought by tourism and the resulting land boom that has turned much of Branson to asphalt.

The rock sits on the side of Pine Mountain, just as it did a century and a half ago and for ages, keeping a lonely vigil over the valley that still bears the ruts of the Forsyth-to-Springdale coach road. It is located about thirty yards east of JJ Highway south of Kirbyville, just a few miles from the heart of downtown Branson. I have seen the location myself, aided by a local historian who had known the location since his childhood.

The rock was as Gamble had described—massive, brooding, and broken into three pieces. Its weathered surface was caked with lichen. On the ground nearby was the hollow stone that Gamble had scooped rainwater from upon his first encounter with

Murder Rock, and where he had placed the bullfrog pipe upon his departure.

The historian was careful to caution that Murder Rock now is on private land and therefore inaccessible to the public. But I captured the coordinates on a handheld GPS unit and, during the making of this book, returned for a little clandestine research.

I parked my Jeep well off the highway atop Pine Mountain, slung a backpack over my shoulder, and hiked down until I found the rock again, nearly hidden by the fiery autumn leaves of the trees. It was late in the afternoon, the sun was slanting through the trees, and I walked around the base of the rock until I found the hollow stone that collects rainwater. Overcoming my fear of snakes, I plunged my hand into the hole, but felt nothing in the bottom except rocks.

I then climbed the fortress's upper tier and surveyed the valley below.

The twenty-first century seemed very far away.

I removed a fiddle and bow from the backpack. Sometime back I had become interested in traditional American music, and had sought out the help of a violin teacher, who taught me enough to play a few simple tunes. I planted my feet, nestled the fiddle against my cheek, and offered my best rendition of "Star of the County Down" to the ghost of Jacob Gamble.

If Jacob heard it, he gave no sign.

As to Alf Bolin, I can only offer this advice: If y find yourself hiking the woods of Taney Count one evening, with a full moon rising, yo speak his name gently, if at all.

Turn the page for an exciting preview of

THE LAST GUNFIGHTER: Avenger
by *William W. Johnstone*
*with J. A. Johnstone*


Coming in March 2007 wherever
Pinnacle Books are sold.

# One

Once, for a brief moment in time, this place had been a boomtown, a trail-drive town, the railhead where thousands upon thousands of cattle had been loaded on trains to begin their long journey to the slaughterhouses of Chicago.

But then the railhead had moved on farther west, taking the hell-on-wheels with it, and in the twenty-some-odd years since then, the town had settled down into a sleepy little farming community where nothing much ever happened.

On this Tuesday morning, that was all about to change.

Six men rode in about eight o'clock. The east-bound train was due at nine. The men tied their horses at the hitch rack in front of the depot and walked across the street to the hash house run by the Chinaman, Ling Wo. They had flapjacks, scrambled eggs and bacon, and coffee as they sat at a table and talked quietly among themselves. Nobody paid much attention to them. At first glance they were ordinary-looking men.

That was because their coats covered the butts of their six-guns. Those guns gleamed with care, and the walnut grips were well worn from long use.

The men took their time eating. Around five minutes to nine, one of them took out a big fancy pocket watch, flipped it open, and checked the time. He looked around the table at the other men, nodded, and snapped the watch closed. As he stood up, he slipped the timepiece back in his pocket. The other men got to their feet as well.

The purposeful way in which they moved toward the door of the hash house was the first hint that something might be wrong. The strangers were brisk and businesslike now. As they stepped out of the building, the sound of a train whistle came clearly through the morning air. The eastbound was on schedule.

Hell, it was even a couple of minutes early.

The men crossed the dusty street to their horses and shucked Winchester repeaters from saddle boots. Then they walked around the red-brick depot building to the platform, instead of going through the lobby. A few townspeople stood on the platform, waiting to either board the train or meet somebody who was getting off. Some of them glanced curiously at the strangers.

A couple of older men, who had been to see the elephant a time or two in their lives, looked with narrowed eyes at the strangers and then turned to walk quickly into the depot, as if they were getting out of the way of something.

The train was in sight now, chugging steadily toward the station from the west, black smoke rising from the diamond-shaped stack on the big

Baldwin locomotive. The man who had checked his watch stepped to the edge of the platform, leaned out slightly to peer along the tracks, and then nodded in satisfaction. He turned to the other five and repeated the nod.

Inside the station, one of the old-timers was talking quickly and earnestly to the stationmaster. The stationmaster frowned dubiously at first, but after a minute he nodded and gestured to one of the boys who worked at the depot. He gave some quick instructions to the boy, who then hurried across the lobby, banged through the doors, and took off at a run down the street, in the direction of the marshal's office.

He wasn't going to get there in time. The train was already pulling into the station.

Frank Morgan's long legs were stretched out in front of him and his hat was tipped down over his eyes. He never slept very well on a train, so earlier that morning, after he'd gotten some coffee and a bite to eat in the dining car, he'd returned to his seat for a nap. He didn't fall completely asleep, but he rested a little while remaining alert. That habitual caution was ingrained so deeply within him that it would always be a part of him, he supposed.

When the train began to slow, Frank felt it and raised his head. He opened his eyes and saw the conductor coming along the aisle. The conductor called out the name of the town where the train was about to stop. It didn't mean much to Frank. The train was somewhere in Kansas; that was all he knew.

Frank thumbed his hat back on thick dark hair streaked liberally with gray. He wore a faded blue work shirt with the sleeves rolled up a little on his muscular forearms. The legs of his denim trousers hung outside the tops of well-worn horseman's boots.

His clothes might be nondescript, but his ruggedly handsome face possessed a power that sometimes made folks look twice at him. He didn't appear to be a wealthy man—but he was. One of the richest hombres west of the Mississippi, in fact, with business interests scattered from the Rio Grande to the Canadian border. Frank Morgan didn't pay much attention to those business interests, though. He had a whole passel of lawyers and accountants in Denver and San Francisco to do that. He watched them just closely enough to know that nobody was trying to cheat him.

No, judging by appearances, Frank Morgan was little more than a saddle tramp. A drifter.

But the Colt Peacemaker on his hip told a different story. He wasn't just *a* drifter. He was *The* Drifter. A fast gun whose fame had spread across the frontier for years. A gunfighter in an era when civilization was on the ascent and men such as Frank Morgan mostly had been bypassed by time.

Not completely, though. Frank wasn't obsolete just yet.

The conductor knew who he was and approached him with obviously mixed emotions. Frank could have sat on the board of directors of this railroad if he had chosen to do so, which meant the conductor had to treat him with some deference. However, Frank was a known killer who had gunned down countless men, and that made him an abomination to the conductor's civilized nature. In the end, the man's respect for money won out over his distaste for violence, and he forced a polite smile onto his face as he asked, "Everything all right this morning, Mr. Morgan?"

"Just fine," Frank said quietly in a deep, controlled voice. The train lurched a little as its brakes began to take hold. "We going to be stopped here long?"

"No, sir, just long enough to take on any passengers and freight we've got waiting for us."

Frank nodded. "Long enough for me to get out and stretch my legs a little, though? I'm a mite stiff after last night."

"We would have been happy to find a sleeping berth for you, Mr. Morgan—"

"You mean you would have kicked somebody out of a berth they had reserved," Frank cut in. He shook his head. "I'll sit up all the way to Chicago before I'll do that."

"Well, ah, in answer to your question, we'll be stopped here for at least five minutes if you want to walk around a little."

"Thanks."

The conductor moved on as the train rocked to a stop. Frank glanced over through the windows by the seats on the other side of the aisle. That was the side the station platform was on. He saw six men standing there with rifles in their hands. As Frank watched, the group split up, three going toward the front of the car, three toward the rear.

"Oh, hell," he said softly.

He came swiftly and smoothly to his feet, his brain already racing as he decided on his course of action. The vestibule at the rear of the car was closer, so he turned in that direction. He wanted to get out of the railroad car as quickly as possible, out where he would have more room to move and where not as many innocents would be endangered by the lead that was about to fly.

Several people turned their heads to look as Frank strode down the aisle. He heard a few startled mutters behind him as some of the passengers realized that something might be wrong. Then he reached the vestibule, stepped through it, and out onto the car's rear platform. His hand was already reaching for the Peacemaker on his hip as he turned toward the station platform.

The three rifle-toters got there at the same time. Their eyes widened as they looked up at him and saw that he was ready for them. One of the men yelled, "Rance! He's back here!"

Then they jerked their rifles up.

Frank's Colt whispered from leather. He fired from the hip, putting a bullet in the chest of the man who had shouted. The lead punched the man backward a couple of steps before he lost his balance and fell.

Frank turned slightly and fired again, so fast that none of the riflemen had had a chance to get a shot off yet. His second bullet shattered the shoulder of a would-be killer and sent the man spinning off his feet.

The third man managed to fire the rifle in his hands, but he rushed the shot and the bullet spanked off the brass fitting at the corner of the railroad car. Frank's Colt blasted a third time. The last of the gunmen who had come in this direction doubled over as the slug tore agonizingly into his belly. He dropped his rifle, clutched his stomach, folded up, and collapsed on the station platform as blood welled over his fingers.

Frank spun around and leaped off the other side of the train. He landed agilely and dropped into a crouch. There was open ground on this side of the train, and no place to hunt some cover. He ran toward the front of the car, bending low.

As he ran, he glanced underneath the car, hoping to spot the legs of the other three men who wanted to kill him so that he could tell what they were doing. All he could see, though, was the raised station platform.

He had nearly reached the front of the car when two of the assassins bounded across the platform at the back of it and began firing at him. He whirled toward them and went to one knee, squeezing off a couple of shots as he crouched.

One of the riflemen lurched, blood spurting from the side of his neck where Frank's bullet had ripped it open. He stumbled around wildly for a second before falling in a limp sprawl.

The other man was hit in the body, but somehow he managed to stay on his feet and keep firing. His aim was none too accurate. Bullets from the Winchester whistled over Frank's head.

Frank's problem now was that the gun in his hand was empty. Under normal circumstances, like riding on a train, he carried it with the hammer resting on an empty chamber, and he had expended all five rounds that the cylinder held. There were fresh cartridges in the loops on his belt, but he would need a few seconds to reload, preferably when slugs weren't coming so close to him that he could hear the wind-rip of their passage beside his ear.

He threw himself to the side, rolled over the rail and under the train. The rough gravel of the roadbed poked at him through his shirt. Coming to rest on his belly, he opened the revolver's cylinder, dumped the empties, and reached behind him to pluck live rounds from the loops of the shell belt. As he began to thumb them into the cylinders, he heard a man shout over the low rumble of the engine, "The bastard's under the train, Rance!"

"Well, find him, damn it!" came the reply in a harsh, gravelly voice.

Frank snapped the Colt's cylinder closed and crawled toward the rear of the car. The sound of the engine would cover up the crunching of the gravel underneath him as he moved. He looked over and saw the booted feet of the man who was searching for him. The gunman was moving slowly and carefully toward the front of the car. Frank could have broken his ankle with a shot, but instead he planned to wait until the assassin had gone on by, then roll out behind him.

That plan fell apart before it had a chance to develop. The rumble of the engine suddenly got louder, and the drivers clattered as they engaged. The train began to move, rolling slowly eastward. Frank's cover was leaving.

The leader of the killers, the man called Rance, must have run up to the engine and climbed into the locomotive's cab. A gun at the engineer's head would force him to move the train.

Frank jammed his gun back in its holster and rolled onto his back. He probably had time to slip out from under the car before the train started moving too fast, but instead he reached up and grabbed hold of the undercarriage. He lifted his feet and twisted his ankles around a pipe. As he pulled himself up, he came clear of the roadbed. The train carried him along as he hung on tightly.

He clung there like a burr until he judged that the caboose was clear of the station. Then he dropped off, timing his move so that he would fall between cross-ties and ignoring the pain that shot through him as his back jolted heavily against the roadbed. The rest of the train passed over him, and when its shade was gone, the morning sunlight jabbed abruptly against Frank's eyes. He squinted and rolled onto his belly again, drawing his gun as he did so.

The man he had wounded a few moments earlier was standing beside the tracks, across from the station platform, looking around in confusion. Clearly, he had expected to find Frank lying in the roadbed once the train was gone.

"Hey!" Frank called.

The man whirled toward him, bringing up the rifle, but before he even started to line up a shot, the Peacemaker in Frank's hand cracked. The range was a little long for a handgun, but Frank had plenty of experience at making such shots.

The slug thudded into the killer's chest and drove him backward as if he had been punched by a giant fist. His arms went up in the air and the Winchester flew from suddenly nerveless fingers. He crashed down beside the steel rails.

With that threat disposed of, Frank leaped to his feet and turned toward the train.

He saw immediately that he'd been a little too

slow. Rance had already climbed down from the cab of the locomotive, bringing the engineer with him. He had his left arm looped tightly around the man's neck, and his right hand held a pistol with the muzzle pressed hard against the engineer's head.

"Drop your gun, Morgan!" Rance yelled as he forced the engineer closer to Frank. "Drop it or I swear I'll blow this poor bastard's brains out!"

# Two

Frank tried not to look into the engineer's eyes, which were wide with terror. Instead, he kept his gaze fixed on the gunman and said, "You know I can't do that, Rance."

"You know me?" Rance looked a little surprised at that.

As a matter of fact, Frank had never seen the man before. He had seen the type, though, too many times to count. A hired gun, a cold-blooded killer. Maybe a little smarter than the run-of-the-mill shootist, judging by the way he'd had his men approach the train. But in the end he was just another gunman.

Frank didn't say that. He said, "Sure. I know if I drop my gun, you'll ventilate me a second later. So I can't do it."

Rance pressed harder on the engineer's temple with the gun barrel. "I'll kill him!"

Frank's shoulders rose and fell in a minuscule shrug. "That's too damned bad, isn't it? Maybe what you should do is drop *your* gun. Your boys are lying back there at the station, either dead or shot up so bad they're out of this fight, and I'll wager that the local law is on its way. But you haven't done anything today that's a hanging offense. You haven't killed anybody. So unless you're wanted for something else, you can surrender and live through this, Rance."

There was no emotion on Rance's weathered, rugged face. "The hell with that," he said. "I took money to do a job. I aim to do it."

"Took money from who?" Frank asked. He had a pretty good idea of what the answer was, but some confirmation of his hunch would be nice.

"Go to hell, gunfighter."

"I hope you enjoyed spending Dutton's money," Frank said.

The slight widening of Rance's eyes told Frank that he'd been right about who hired the killers. Then Rance jerked his gun toward Frank and fired.

The shot went wild because the gun in The Drifter's hand had roared a shaved instant of time earlier. Frank's bullet had already sizzled past the engineer's ear, aimed at the narrow slice of Rance's face that Frank could see. It struck Rance in the right eye and bored on into his brain just as the gunman pulled the trigger. The .45 slug went all the way through and burst out the back of Rance's skull in a spray of blood, bone splinters, and gray matter. He stood there for a second with his arm still around the engineer's neck before the rest of his body caught up with the fact that he was dead. Then he let go, slid down to his knees, and toppled onto his side.

The engineer fell the other direction, passing

out from fear and strain and the sudden relief of realizing that he was still alive.

Before Frank could holster his gun, a man's voice called from behind him, "Drop it! Drop that gun, mister! I got a scattergun pointed right at you!"

Frank didn't move. He asked, "Are you the law?"

"That's right. I'm the town marshal here, and I got a shotgun and two deputies that're armed too. You gonna put that gun down, or do we have to shoot?"

"Take it easy, Marshal," Frank said. He bent forward and carefully placed the Colt on the roadbed. Then he straightened and lifted both hands to shoulder lever. "I'm turning around now."

"Do it slow and careful-like, and don't try nothin' funny."

Frank did as he was told, saw that the marshal was a stocky, middle-aged man with graying red hair. He was flanked by a couple of much younger and more nervous deputies. They worried Frank more than the marshal did. The local badge had the look of an experienced man who wouldn't panic and start shooting unless he had good reason to.

"It's all over, Marshal," Frank said, keeping his voice calm and steady. "Why don't you tell your deputies to lower those Greeners? I'd hate for one of them to go off accidentally."

"Won't be nothin' accidental about it if you try anything," the lawman warned.

"I'm not going to. All I did was defend myself. Those men met the train with the sole intention of killing me. They were hired guns."

The marshal frowned. "Who the hell are you,

that somebody would send six bushwhackers after you?"

"My name is Frank Morgan."

That meant something to all three of the star-packers. The eyes of the younger men got even wider. "Hell, he's The Drifter!" one of the deputies exclaimed. "He's in some o' those yellowbacks I read!"

Frank tried not to sigh. Not for the first time, he thought there ought to be a law against pasty-faced scribblers making up a bunch of rubbish about real people and publishing it in dime novels.

"The Drifter, eh?" the marshal said. Without taking his eyes off Frank, he ordered his deputies, "Lower those scatterguns. Unless he's got another gun hid somewhere on him, he's unarmed, and I ain't never heard nothin' about Frank Morgan carryin' a hideout." The lawman tucked his own Greener under his arm. "Now, what's all this about, Morgan?"

"I'd be glad to come down to your office and tell you all about it, Marshal, but only if you can convince the conductor to hold the train for me. I don't want to have to wait until the next eastbound comes through to be on my way."

"I'll see what I can do . . . but don't forget, you ain't the one givin' the orders here." The marshal turned his head and snapped at one of the deputies, "Go check on them fellas who got shot. Some of 'em might still be alive. Josh, you go fetch the doc." As the deputies hurried to carry out the commands, the marshal asked Frank, "Did Endicott get hit?"

"Who?"

"Cleve Endicott. The engineer."

"Oh." Frank shook his head. "No, I don't think he's hurt. Looked to me like he just fainted."

For the first time, a hint of amusement appeared on the lawman's rugged face. "Swooned like a gal, eh? He'll get some ribbin' about that. I might've done the same thing, though. I saw that shot you made just as I was gettin' here. That bullet couldn't have missed him by much more'n an inch."

"That was enough," Frank said.

The marshal grunted. "Yeah. Come on, Morgan. Let's go talk to the conductor."

The conductor didn't like holding the train, but he agreed to for half an hour. The engineer had to be brought around, anyway, and given a little while to recover from his fainting spell.

The marshal, whose name was Harry Larch, walked down to his office with Frank. Larch had Frank's Colt tucked behind his belt, and Frank had retrieved his hat from the roadbed, where it had fallen off.

As he brushed dirt from the Stetson and settled it on his head, he asked, "Am I under arrest?"

"Not yet. I just want some answers, is all. There hasn't been any real trouble here in my town for a long time, and I want to know why folks started dyin' this morning all of a sudden."

The dying hadn't started this morning, Frank thought. This was just the latest installment.

The marshal's office was in a small, blocky building

that also served as the town jail. A coffeepot sat on a cast-iron stove in the corner. After putting the shotgun back on the rack, Larch offered Frank a cup, and Frank accepted gratefully.

"I used to do some cowboying, and that's where I learned to boil coffee," the marshal said. "So this is pretty potent."

Frank smiled. "Just the way I like it."

Larch poured coffee for both of them and waved Frank into a chair in front of the battered, scarred desk. He took Frank's gun from behind his belt and placed it on the desk. As he settled down in a swivel chair, he said, "Now tell me why somebody wants you dead, Morgan . . . other than the fact that a man like you must have a lot of enemies to start with."

Frank took a sip of the strong black brew and nodded in appreciation. Then he said, "Those gunmen were sent to intercept me by a man in Boston named Charles Dutton."

"Why would this fella Dutton do that?"

"Because he knows that I'm on my way to Boston to kill *him*."

Larch's bushy eyebrows rose in surprise. "Simple as that, eh?"

Frank nodded. "Simple as that."

But it wasn't simple, not really. Not at all. And the beginnings of it went back years. Maybe even decades, depending on how you looked at it.

It went all the way back to when he had met and fallen in love with and ultimately married a beautiful young woman named Vivian. Her father had been opposed to the marriage, and eventually had succeeded in having it set aside legally. But he couldn't do anything about the child Vivian had been carrying when she and Frank parted, and even though Vivian had wound up marrying somebody else who had raised her son Conrad as his own, the boy was Frank's and that connection would always exist between them.

Years later, they had met again. Vivian Browning was a widow by this time, and a very rich widow, to boot. It was then that Frank had learned for the first time he had a son. Conrad Browning's dislike for Frank had made his reunion with Vivian a bittersweet one, but given enough time, things might have improved all around.

They didn't get the chance to, because Vivian had been betrayed and set up by one of her attorneys, a man named Charles Dutton. Because of Dutton's treachery, Vivian had been cut down by an outlaw's bullet, ending her life and driving a wedge between Frank and Conrad that threatened to become permanent.

Fate had cast the two men together again on several occasions, and Conrad had overcome his resentment of his true father to form a grudging respect for Frank. They had even worked together to ward off threats to a railroad Conrad was building down in New Mexico Territory. They were partners whether they wanted to be or not, since Vivian's will had left a large share of her business holdings to Frank and the rest to Conrad.

Frank had met Charles Dutton briefly, before Vivian's death. He knew the man was responsible for what had happened, even though Dutton hadn't actually pulled the trigger himself, and he was aware that Dutton had fled back to Boston. Frank had intended to go after him and settle the score, but other things had gotten in the way, keeping him from getting around to it.

And then, while Frank was embroiled in a bloody range war down Arizona way, a hired killer had come after him and forced a showdown. Frank had emerged triumphant from that shoot-out. As the gunman lay dying, he had revealed that Charles Dutton had hired him to kill Frank. Clearly, Dutton felt that Frank's very existence posed too much of a continuing threat and had decided to have him eliminated.

Instead, the attempt on his life had served as a wake-up call for Frank, a reminder that he had unfinished business to take care of. Now he was on his way East, and nothing was going to sidetrack him until he had looked into Charles Dutton's eyes and avenged Vivian's death.

He quickly sketched in this background for Marshal Harry Larch, then said, "I suspect Dutton has spies keeping an eye on me. I rode from Arizona up to Denver and talked to my lawyers there, made arrangements for my horse and my dog to be taken care of while I was gone, and bought a train ticket to Boston. I see now that was a mistake, though."

"How come?" Larch asked, clearly fascinated by Frank's story.

"How come it was a mistake? Because if Dutton knows that I'm coming for him—and I'm sure he does—he'll do his damnedest to try to stop me. He'll try to have me killed before I can get anywhere close to him. He's got the money to hire plenty of gunmen, too . . . money he stole from my late wife."

"What's that got to do with you riding the train?"

"I'm an easy target on a train," Frank explained. "There's no room to move, and there are too many innocent people around. Not only that, but the men who are after me will always know where to find me." He shook his head. "What I've got to do is throw them off the trail. That's my best chance of getting to Dutton."

Larch rubbed his jaw and frowned in thought. "Even if you make it to Boston, it won't be easy gettin' to Dutton. He'll probably have himself a bunch o' bodyguards."

"I expect so," Frank said with a calm nod.

"So you're willin' to fight your way through a whole army o' hired guns and guards just to take your shot at this hombre."

"That's about the size of it."

The marshal laced his hands together and leaned back in his chair as his frown darkened. "There's one thing you're forgettin', Morgan. . . . No matter how justified you may feel in seekin' revenge, what you're really talkin' about is murder. This is a civilized country now. You can't just walk up to a man and gun him down, no matter what he's done. If you can prove that Dutton is responsible for your wife's death, you need to go to the law and let them handle it."

Frank nodded. "I wouldn't expect you to tell me any different, Marshal. And what you say would be mighty good advice for most people. But I'm in the habit of stompin' my own snakes, and I reckon I'm too old to change now."

Larch sighed and reached out to rest his hand on Frank's gun. He shoved the Peacemaker across the desk toward The Drifter. "All I can say is that I'm damn sure glad this fella Dutton is in Boston and not here in my town. This is gonna be some other lawman's worry."

# Three

Only one of the hired killers had survived the shoot-out at the train station, the man whose shoulder Frank had broken with a bullet. He was expected to recover from his wound, although in all likelihood he would never have full use of that arm again. Frank and Marshal Larch stopped in at the doctor's office to see the man on their way back to the depot.

The doctor's office was in his house, about a block from the station. The wounded man was propped up in bed with bandages wrapped around his shoulder. One of Larch's deputies sat in a straight chair next to the wall, a shotgun lying across his knees.

The gunman was pale from pain and loss of blood. He had a thin, beard-stubbled face and watery eyes. He didn't look at Frank and the marshal as they came into the room.

Larch said, "In case you ain't figured it out yet, you're under arrest for attempted murder."

"I didn't try to murder nobody," the man muttered

sullenly. Still without looking at Frank, he waved his left hand in The Drifter's general direction. "He's the fella you oughtta be arrestin'. He gunned down my friends for no good reason."

"Other than the fact that you were shootin' at him."

"He shot first," the gunman said accusingly.

Larch glanced over at Frank, who nodded. "As a matter of fact, that's true," Frank admitted. "I saw them through the window and recognized them for what they were. They split up, half of them heading for the front of the car and the other three for the back. I met this man and two others at the back of the car. They pointed their rifles at me and one of them yelled at the leader that I was back there. I figured that was justification enough."

The deputy nodded and said, "That fits with the story Josh and me got from the witnesses, Marshal."

"I never said you weren't justified in what you did, Morgan," Larch said. "I wish you'd picked some other town to shoot up, though." He held up his hands to forestall Frank's response. "I know. It wasn't really your choice, was it?"

The gunman said, "Morgan's a killer. He's killed hundreds of men, from what I've heard. He's the one who oughtta be behind bars."

"I never killed anybody who didn't have it coming," Frank said. "And I'd challenge anybody to prove otherwise."

"Never mind about that," Larch said. "All I'm concerned with is what happened here, and I'm satisfied you acted in self-defense. I'll testify to as much at the inquest, which is the only reason I'm willin' to let you catch that train and leave town." He turned his attention back to the gunman. "Now, who hired you and those other boys to kill Morgan?"

The man's expression grew even more sulky. "Nobody hired us. I don't know what you're talkin' about."

"Was it a man named Dutton?" Larch asked, ignoring the gunman's denial.

Frank was watching the man's eyes closely, and he saw no sign of recognition in them. The gunman had never heard of Charles Dutton. That didn't really come as a surprise. Rance had been the leader of the bunch, and it was entirely possible he was the only one who had known who they were working for.

"This is all crazy," the gunman insisted, refusing to answer Larch's question. "Morgan started shootin' at us for no reason."

Larch nodded wearily. "You just stick to that story, son. We'll see whether or not a jury believes it . . . and then you'll have a nice long time to think about it in prison."

Frank caught the marshal's eye and gave a little shake of his head. Larch was wasting his time. The would-be killer didn't know anything that could be used legally against Dutton. As usual, the slick lawyer had covered his tracks, although it was lucky for Dutton that Rance had been killed in the shooting.

"Stay here and keep an eye on him for now," Larch ordered the deputy. "As soon as the doc says it's all right, we'll move him down to the jail. He can recuperate there while he's waitin' to stand trial."

With that, Frank and the marshal left the doctor's house and walked on to the railroad station. The stationmaster, the conductor, the engineer, and the brakeman were conferring on the platform. They turned to look at the newcomers, and the conductor asked irritably, "Are we about ready to roll again? The head office ain't gonna be happy about us fallin' this far behind schedule."

The stationmaster put in, "I wired on ahead to the next stop so they'd know to expect a delay. Shouldn't cause too much of a problem. Cleve can make up a little time between stops."

The engineer seemed to be none the worse for his perilous experience earlier. He frowned at Frank and said, "Mister, you damned near shot me."

"But I didn't," Frank replied coolly. "When you get right down to cases, that's all that really counts, isn't it?"

The engineer's reply was a grudging, "Maybe. But what if I'd moved my head a little just as you pulled the trigger?"

"That would have been a shame," Frank said. "I was counting on you being too scared to move."

The engineer glared, but didn't make any reply to that. He looked at the other men and said, "I've got steam up. Let's get the hell outta here."

Frank went back to the passenger car where he had been riding earlier. As he found a seat, he felt the eyes of the other passengers watching him. They had been talking animatedly among themselves about the gun battle they had witnessed, but they fell silent as Frank walked past them. Everybody in here now knew that the notorious gunslinger known as The Drifter was among them. Some were intrigued and impressed, but most of them were just plain scared. Frank couldn't blame them for feeling that way, either. When they had gotten on this train, they hadn't known that they would be riding with a famous gunfighter with a habit of attracting trouble.

That was truer now than ever. Frank had no doubt that if he remained on this train, he would draw more killers than honey did flies.

About five miles east of the town where the shoot-out had taken place, there was a grade that, while not steep, was long enough to cause the train to slow down a little. At the top of that grade, Frank Morgan tossed the carpetbag he had purchased in Denver from the rear platform of the caboose, and then swung down to the ground himself, running a few steps before he caught his balance and stopped.

He looked up at the caboose, where the conductor stood with his arms crossed and an unfriendly look on his face. Clearly, the conductor was glad to see Frank leave the train, even if it wasn't at a scheduled stop.

As the train chugged on eastward, receding into the distance, Frank picked up his carpetbag and walked in the same direction. Like most men who had spent the greater portion of their lives in the saddle, he didn't care much for walking, but his low-heeled boots didn't hurt his feet too much. Besides, he didn't have very far to go. Only a couple of hundred yards ahead was a line of cottonwood trees that marked the course of a creek. That was his destination.

He walked beside the gleaming steel rails until he reached the creek, which was spanned by a short trestle. Moving under the trees, he found a log where he could sit down and wait with his carpetbag at his feet. The shade was welcome. The sun had risen high enough by now that the day was beginning to heat up.

Frank had been waiting only about half an hour when he heard the hoofbeats of several horses approaching. He stood up and turned toward the sound. Out of habit, his hand hovered near the butt of the gun on his hip. After a moment, he relaxed as he recognized the man riding toward the creek and leading two horses behind him.

Marshal Harry Larch rode into the trees and brought his mount to a halt. He swung down from the saddle and handed the reins of the two riderless horses to Frank.

Larch said, "I'm damned if I know why I'm doin' this, Morgan. I ought to arrest you, considerin' the errand you're on." He shrugged. "But I'm old enough to remember a time when the only law west of the Mississippi was what a man packed on his hip. Those were worse times in a lot of ways . . . but by God, I'm not convinced that justice wasn't better served back then, too."

"That's one of the burdens of getting older, Marshal," Frank told him. "You see too many changes, good and bad." He looked over the horses Larch had brought him. Both were geldings. One was a rangy lineback dun with a bit of a mean cast to his eyes; the other a sturdy chestnut with a white blaze and three white stockings. The dun was saddled, while the chestnut had several bags full of supplies slung over its back.

Frank transferred the contents of his carpetbag

to the saddlebags on the dun, then handed the empty carpetbag to Larch and said, "If you know anybody who can make good use of that, they're welcome to it."

"Hell, it's nearly brand-new."

"I'm used to traveling light," Frank said with a shrug.

"And money don't mean a whole lot to you, does it? With what you gave me back in town, I was able to pay the livery owner a good price for these horses."

"Anybody who claims money doesn't matter has never been without it," Frank said. "I know what it's like to be poor. I have been, plenty of times in my life. But I also know that money's real value is in what it can accomplish. I'd spend every penny I have if it helped me settle the score with Dutton."

Larch grimaced. "Just take the horses—you paid for 'em—and don't remind me that you're on your way to kill a man."

Frank nodded. He put his foot in the stirrup and swung up into the dun's saddle. Then he reached down and held out his hand to Larch. The marshal hesitated for a second, but then took it in a firm grip.

"I don't know whether to wish you luck or not," Larch said gruffly, "but I reckon I hope you don't get *yourself* killed, Morgan."

"I'll settle for that," Frank replied with a grin. "So long, Marshal."

As he rode out from under the trees, Frank thought he heard Larch mutter *"Vaya con Dios"* behind him.

\* \* \*

It wouldn't be long before Dutton heard about the shoot-out at the railroad station. In these days of telegraphic communication, news could travel hundreds of miles, even thousands, in no time at all. It was even possible that Dutton had an agent on the same train as Frank, keeping an eye on him.

But even if that was the case, no one would know for sure that Frank was no longer on board until the train reached the next town. No one except Marshal Larch and the train's conductor, that is, and Frank didn't think either of them would reveal what they knew. Frank had worked out the plan with Larch and given the marshal money to buy the horses and supplies, and not until the train was already moving had Frank sought out the conductor and explained to him what he was going to do. That had been fine with the conductor, who was happy to see Frank gone before more trouble broke out.

Of course, it was going to take a lot longer to reach Boston on horseback than it would by rail, but that delay couldn't be avoided. Besides, Frank thought, he sort of liked the idea that Dutton would have longer to wait and worry this way. Maybe it was a little malicious to feel like that—but Frank thought that his grief over Vivian's death had earned him the right to feel some malice toward Dutton.

He cut north from the railroad, heading for the low, rolling mounds of the Smoky Hills. He wasn't quite sure just how a fella would go about riding a horse all the way to Boston, but he supposed that if he kept heading in the right general direction, he would get there sooner or later.

By nightfall, he was a long way from where he had left the train, and he wondered if Dutton had found out by now what had happened.

Frank found a good place to camp among the hills, next to a small stream. He unsaddled the dun and took the supplies off the chestnut and hobbled both horses. If he'd been riding his stallion Stormy, he would have just turned him loose, knowing that Stormy wouldn't stray far. As he built a small fire and settled down to fry some bacon, he thought about Stormy and the big cur called Dog, and he hoped both of the animals were doing all right back in Denver. He wouldn't have left them behind if he had known how things were going to work out, but at the time he had planned to travel all the way to Boston on the train and had figured that having the animals along would only complicate things, especially once he reached the city.

The biggest towns Frank had ever seen were New Orleans, St. Louis, and San Francisco, although Denver was starting to get some pretty good size to it. He wondered what Boston would be like. The thought of being surrounded by thousands and thousands of people made him a little uneasy. Not only that, but he had heard that there were towns *everywhere* back East, instead of just every so often along the trail. Thinking about that made Frank shake his head. He wasn't sure why folks would want to live like that. He'd have trouble breathing if he couldn't get out away from everybody else once in a while . . . like in these Smoky Hills of Kansas.

Which were about to get more crowded, he realized suddenly as he lifted his head and listened to

the sound of hoofbeats that came out of the night.
Riders . . .

A lot of them, from the sound of it, and they were
coming fast.

# More Western Adventures
# From Karl Lassiter

**First Cherokee Rifles**

              0-7860-1008-8          **$5.99**US/**$7.99**CAN

**The Battle of Lost River**

              0-7860-1191-2          **$5.99**US/**$7.99**CAN

**White River Massacre**

              0-7860-1436-9          **$5.99**US/**$7.99**CAN

**Warriors of the Plains**

              0-7860-1437-7          **$5.99**US/**$7.99**CAN

**Sword and Drum**

              0-7860-1572-1          **$5.99**US/**$7.99**CAN

*Available Wherever Books Are Sold!*

Visit our website at **www.kensingtonbooks.com**.

# THE MOUNTAIN MAN SERIES BY
# WILLIAM W. JOHNSTONE